The Atlas Legacy

Colin Newton

Onwards and Upwards Publishers,
Berkeley House,
11 Nightingale Crescent,
West Horsley,
Surrey,
KT24 6PD

www.onwardsandupwards.org

ISBN: 978-1-910197-80-6

Printed in the UK
by 4edge Limited

Contents

1. An Ancient Secret 5

2. A Team Meets Up 15

3. The Puzzle Outlined 21

4. Plans 29

5. Valley of the Iceman 36

6. Cornwall 42

7. Hania 49

8. Aftermath 61

9. Clues 71

10. Blessing 81

11. Journey 88

12. Malta 94

13. Look to the East 104

14. Discovery 113

15. Review 124

16. Back Home 135

1

An Ancient Secret

Two tall men stood together on a slight rise in the rocky Mediterranean coast, looking out east at the full moon rising above the water. Behind them stretched a long and almost featureless climb to the island's interior, over which the sun was now setting. The western sky was bright red. There was a lot of dust in the atmosphere, so sunsets had been spectacular all summer. This was the last day of their assignment. The ship to take them back home was waiting in a deep and sheltered bay, half a mile to the south. Beneath their feet, concealed, was the result of the labours they had supervised.

The older man, dark and craggy featured, bearing healed-over scars of battle on his face and arms, looked out over the waves towards the moon. He spoke in an archaic form of Greek, fluently yet with a trace of occasional hesitation, as if the tongue, though familiar, was not his native language. "It is fitting we should end today. The symbol of our king and our great captain rises in the direction whence we go. So it was when I was last here."

His younger companion looked surprised. "You have been here before? I thought this island was enemy territory until the disaster."

"It was. I do not doubt that in the great bays north and south of here were assembled the fleet and army that assailed us. They are gone now, the sea kings swallowed by their own element. So our

5

lord guessed when he sent us here that this coast would prove deserted. But back then…" He paused, remembering. "We heard the news too late that Atlas had invaded this island. We could not prevent it, so close to his bases and so far from ours. But when the wind set in from the north east, our captain realised that the enemy ships were pinned in the very harbours that sheltered them. So we swept down unopposed on the southern side of the bay yonder." He waved southwards, indicating where a curve in the coast was just visible. "We found refugees from the sword of Atlas, penned on to that peninsula as their last refuge. We were able to rescue them and bring them safe to Athens."

"I wish I could have gone on some of those rescues," said the younger man wistfully. He had not taken part in the warfare now ended, except for the last defence when all were summoned to their king's side. He was unsure whether the prospect of a more peaceful life pleased him by its lack of danger, or saddened him by having no need for deeds of daring.

"Yes, they were quite an experience. The stealthy plotting of a route into territory where the enemy threatened, the careful tactics and sudden massing of our forces giving us an advantage, the delight and relief on the faces of the faithful when they saw us arrive; the fear in our opponents' faces, when the banner was raised and they realised what captain they were facing. We were the refuge for all who fled from evil in those years. Even our king; he once dwelt in the mountains of the lands north of here, and escaped when his father and grandparents were slain by the hordes of Atlas. That is all over now, of course. The tribes of the dispossessed are returned to their homelands in safety, and our tongues are sundered so we cannot rebuild what is gone."

"It is well, nonetheless," replied the younger man, "for the threat of our enemies is gone for ever. Their armies also are scattered across the globe, those that survived, and cannot be marshalled again. That danger is gone."

"I wonder," said the older man, frowning. "Our king does not think so, not gone for ever. There was a prophecy he received not long before the end: 'Store the story of this hour, against the time

6

when the servants of the serpent again seek dominion.' It is said truly that our Lord shall crush his head, but the serpent shall also inflict a wound before that time comes. It may be that again the faithful shall dwell in fear.

"But hopefully not in our time," he continued more cheerfully. "Just as the years stretched out when Noah was bearing witness, and some died in peace rather than in the flood waters, so we may hope that our days will be peaceful now. But the next generation, or the one following, or maybe a hundred from now... Evil will find a way to rear its head again."

They inspected the slope around them for the last time as the daylight slowly faded. "It doesn't look like anyone's ever been here," said the younger man.

"That's how it's supposed to look," his companion reminded him. They both smiled. Then they turned and walked along the coast to their waiting ship, hurrying in case the darkness descended before they reached camp. The land behind was deserted. It would keep its secret through thousands of years.

Seb Lowry glanced at the map beside him yet again. If he'd been less frustrated, he would have appreciated the irony – a seasoned traveller on five continents, lost in the outskirts of his own capital city. But time was pressing and the London backstreets seemed as impenetrable as a rainforest. He was sure he'd been down this one at least twice already. Perhaps the next left turn? No, he'd already tried that. Why hadn't he brought his satnav? His sudden change of mind drew a critical horn blast from the car behind. Straight on, then. The next turning? No, a 'no entry' sign loomed. The third turning looked like new ground. Left, then right. A hundred yards on; at last there was the street he'd been looking for.

Finding a parking space took a few minutes more. Finally he stood outside a modern-looking building. Red brick, rather than stone, wasn't how he thought a church would look, but the name on the noticeboard matched the one in his notes. Still he hesitated briefly. It was a long time since he'd been inside a church. He checked the service times; he was late, the evening service would have been going for twenty minutes already. He guessed that this would make it easier to slip in unnoticed, which suited him fine. Well, the person he wanted to see should be inside, so he'd better go in too.

Seb pushed the door open and a surprised steward rose to greet the latecomer. A few heads turned and saw the stranger, then quickly switched attention back to the service. One teenager did a double take. Seb moved quietly to a seat at the back of the hall, scanning the room as he did so. He had expected pews and a pulpit; an elderly, well-dressed congregation. Instead he saw plastic chairs, a stage at the front, and musicians with drums and guitars. There were more people than he had expected, more young people especially. Fashionable clothes too; he was overdressed in a suit. He couldn't see the one face he might recognize.

To his surprise and relief, the man leading the meeting – from some dim memory Seb recalled the title of 'pastor' – immediately answered his unspoken question. "Now we welcome our new graduate back from Reading."

Seb joined in warm applause as on to the stage stepped the tallish, athletic brunette he remembered, still in student garb of faded jeans and T-shirt. He recalled their first meeting, just over a year before. On that occasion he had been the one on a platform, speaking to an enthralled audience. It had all gone so well until he had taken questions from the floor. To have one of his key arguments demolished by an undergraduate...

Seb had emerged from that encounter more interested than dismayed. He loved a good argument, the chance to hone his theories against the steel of an equally keen and well-informed mind. He had kept in touch with the young woman who had floored him. She was less keen on their ongoing correspondence, though in one rather optimistic moment she had tried to get him to attend an outreach meeting at her church. He had passed up that invite, but kept the information for reference. Now he had shown up, with a surprise of his own in mind.

Bethany Fisher, BSc (Archaeology), thanked her friends for their love, prayers and support over the last three years. She went on to tell of what "the Lord was doing" at the university: people who had become Christians in recent months, the most recent another finalist only three days from the end of her course; a friend on the French course, anxious about finding fellowship in her year abroad, had been led to link up with a couple planting a church; continuing plans for evangelising the campus, in which some of the newest converts were set to play the keenest part; guidance in finding jobs or accommodation for the next term.

"Praise the Lord!" chorused several members of the congregation.

Seb found himself wondering how someone so intelligent could talk about the supernatural with such clear sincerity. Where was the blind spot in her mind… or could the error be his in discounting the divine? Then a change of subject grabbed his attention.

"The one person God doesn't seem to have sorted out is me. Perhaps you could pray that Arsenal Ladies will give me another chance. Or that someone would just walk in here and offer me a job."

Seb had never thought of himself as an answer to prayer.

For the remainder of the service, Seb was waiting impatiently. He paid little attention to the singing, except to note that it was livelier than he had expected. Maybe he would have kept up his teenage flirtation with religion if he'd found a church like this one. His only interest in the sermon was to appreciate the minister's ability to sustain audience attention. As an occasional public speaker himself, that was within his compass.

The benediction was given and the service ended. As people began to move around and chat, Seb rose and started towards the coffee table. A tall, excited, and rather incredulous teenager blocked his path. "Seb Lowry? I'm Josiah Hope. I saw your Ancient Quest series on Discovery, and I've read the book. What brings you here?"

Seb was always happy to oblige a fan. He pulled a document from his briefcase and unfolded it.

Josiah's eyes widened. "One of the ancient maps you described in your book?"

"Yes – well, a copy," confirmed Seb, pointing to features one by one. "Turkish, like the Piri Re'is map I described, but about forty years later, and much more complete. As you've read Ancient Quest, you will know that the Turkish admiral Piri Re'is, just twenty-one years after Columbus' first voyage, somehow plotted parts of America that had not yet been explored. Not content with that, he drew part of Antarctica, three hundred years before modern people reached it. He claimed, as I said in my book, that he had access to ancient source maps – but who drew those?

"That analysis wasn't new, of course – several authors have cited it in recent decades. But this map here is a new find. On this map, you can see most of Europe, parts of America, Africa, the Indian Ocean, more of the Antarctic coastline. The Antarctic is the key, as you'll remember from Ancient Quest. No-one for thousands of years before the sixteenth century had seen the Antarctic, definitely not in the ice-free state that's portrayed, and they could not have mapped it accurately if they had seen it. I believe it's the decisive proof that somewhere out there are the remains of an advanced lost civilization – older and more developed than anything currently in the history books – waiting to be dug up."

Josiah stared at the chart in wonder. "It was fascinating to read about these maps, but to actually see one is, well, something else... Have you had this one analysed?"

Seb nodded. "Longitudes and latitudes check out to a high degree of accuracy. The centre of the plot is in Egypt, at thirty degrees north of the equator. That's typical of this sort of map. Latitude could be measured at the time this map was drawn, but the means to measure longitude was only developed around two centuries later. It's a sixteenth century map that could not have been plotted in the sixteenth century. And look here," he pointed to North America. "These markings denote glaciers. And in Europe it cuts off at about the latitude of London, which is where the limits of the ice would have been. The map is showing Ice Age conditions in the northern hemisphere. That makes it ten thousand years old and more."

Josiah was impressed, but also puzzled. "Why bring the map here?"

Seb grinned. "I want to know what a certain newly-graduated sceptic has to say about this. I think I can solve her worries about job prospects."

"Bethany?" asked Josiah, puzzled. Then he quipped, "Wouldn't her professor's opinion be more valuable?"

"Perhaps, but her professor didn't care enough about my theories to come and challenge me. We had quite a debate on the Reading leg of my 2014 tour. Challenges are much better than indifference – and I don't duck them."

Josiah called and Bethany turned in his direction. But when she saw his companion she stopped short, frowning. Her spat with Seb the previous year had been entertaining, but a would-be serious archaeologist could do without being associated with a maverick Atlantis hunter.

Seb stepped forward and flourished the map. Bethany glared as if it was unworthy of her attention. But she took in Josiah's excited gaze, remembered him plying her with questions at one youth evening. Clearly he had a fascination for this sort of stuff. Maybe a bit of cool professional disparagement would open his eyes, at least. She needed to muster an argument, and for that she needed information. "Where does this come from?"

"The original is in the archives of the National Museum of Malta. It was left behind in the Turkish retreat after the Great Siege of Malta, and kept by the knights of St John. It probably belonged to the Turkish Admiral Piali, who commanded the fleet at the siege. He was a successor of Piri Re'is. This is only a reproduction, of course. The museum still has the original."

Bethany didn't recognise the name of Piri Re'is. Seb repeated the explanation he'd just given to Josiah.

"The museum thinks it's genuine?"

Seb nodded.

"What date?"

"The siege was in 1565. The map is probably from the late 1550s."

Bethany stopped and thought. "OK. So whoever drew this presumably had that earlier map fragment, which you're so keen on, available to them. The American coast here would be partly a copy from – what do you call him? – Re'is, and partly influenced by the sixteenth century explorations. No surprises there. More imaginary islands in the mid-Atlantic, that's pure fiction. The African coast is pretty good, so is India, but that was hardly unknown territory in 1550. The alleged Antarctic bit – I'm sure a proper analysis would show it was a lucky guess. Are you claiming that misshapen blob is Australia?"

Seb came back at once, relishing the debate, confident of his ground. "The projection is centred on Egypt, so you're bound to get distortions when you draw something as far away as Australia. The Australian bit seems to date from the last Ice Age; the land mass includes Papua New Guinea due to lower sea levels. The eastern coast of Australia on the map is actually the right longitude for New Zealand. Obviously the land link between Australia and New Zealand is a mistake. And the Antarctic coast can be verified in the same way as in earlier studies. Of course that has to have been mapped at a different time, during a spell of warm climate."

"I don't keep up on this stuff. Remind me – what earlier studies?" queried Bethany.

"Occasional analyses of mysterious old maps have been around for decades. Even Einstein was intrigued when he heard about them. They've been cited by every ancient mystery hunter from von Daniken to... to Lowry, I suppose." He grinned. "You really should study my book more, you know."

Josiah looked from one to the other, hoping for a resolution to the discussion. Bethany tried to oblige. "You claim that the bits that look accurate are miraculously preserved ancient knowledge. The bits that are obviously wrong are sixteenth century errors. Cavemen are far too clever to make mistakes, no doubt. And by the way, Einstein probably knew as much about map-making as you or I know about nuclear physics." The scorn was becoming clearer with every word. "So, is that your best shot?"

Seb frowned. "You're choosing to overlook that even for known parts of the world, mapping to this accuracy was not possible in the sixteenth century. As I just remarked to your friend here, they had no way of determining longitude. Now, take a look at these notes I've had translated."

Bethany sighed audibly, but looked anyway. Seb pointed to Egypt, then moved his finger over to a linked marginal note. "'Treasures of Thoth … searches have found nothing.' The concept of lost 'Treasures of Thoth' goes back to the early dynasties of Egypt; the Pharaohs tried to find them but failed. They're supposed to be somewhere on the Giza plateau, around or under the pyramids. People are still looking, including me.

"Now here…" Seb pointed to a miniscule dot below Italy, then followed a line linking it to the margin. "Malta. 'Treasures of Zeus'. That's a new concept. I think that the Turks knew that there was something very ancient, and very valuable, hidden on Malta. Part of their purpose in invading was to find it. They were beaten back and never had the chance to make a thorough search. Now I'm taking up the hunt.

"But I want someone with me who will make sure that I do things correctly, so I can't be criticised for jumping to conclusions without considering alternatives. Someone to throw in objection after objection, so that I can refine my case in the fire of heated debate. I believe you've got the intelligence and tenacity to do that. You just said you wanted someone to walk in here and offer you a job. That's why I'm here."

Bethany was startled, amused, but also indignant. Momentarily it occurred to her that the Lord might just have set up this coincidence. She decided to assume he hadn't. If she was wrong, let him show her. "I would prefer a proper job, with potential to advance a career in archaeology. Starting by looking for Atlantis might just kill my career at birth," she remarked dryly.

Seb had expected the negative response, but he tried again. "Only if we fail to find it," he quipped. "Besides, whatever is on

Malta might be nothing to do with Atlantis. I go with the data, not with preconceptions. There is something to be found; I've got other clues to share with you..." He could see he was getting nowhere. "Look, I'm not flying to Malta tomorrow. In a few months' time, I might seem a good alternative to unemployment. My offer is open any time you care to take it up."

Bethany shook her head. "Thanks and all that, but the answer's no. If you'll excuse me, I have friends to catch up with." She walked away.

Josiah steered Seb towards the coffee and biscuits. He was still keen to continue the conversation. "This search of yours. Could you use someone on a gap year between school and university?"

Seb pondered the unexpected suggestion. "I'll have to think about it. Check the budget. It might depend on how well Ancient Quest sales hold up in the rest of the year." An opening occurred to him. "If you did come, might that influence Bethany?"

Josiah was tempted to say yes, but resisted the lie. She was just out of University; why should she choose the company of someone about to start? They both had their own circles of friends. The shared faith and church was almost the only link between them.

Seb nodded reluctantly. "Do you know if she really has a chance with Arsenal Ladies?"

Josiah didn't know, but if there was only one topic that would keep Seb's attention, he might as well spin things out. "Maybe, I guess. I think she may have had a trial as a schoolgirl. She plays for a strong local soccer team, not the top league but not far off. I've heard it said that the amount of time she spent on sport is the only thing that stopped her getting a First."

They chatted for a bit longer, to no great consequence. Seb took Josiah's address and promised to be in touch about the Malta search, but gave no guarantees. It was enough of a possibility to keep Josiah happy.

2

A Team Meets Up

Josiah loved puzzles and he loved history – the older the better. When not busy with his schoolwork and church activities, he'd read widely on ancient mysteries, although as a Christian he avoided works with strong occult flavour to them. Men like Seb Lowry were his heroes – people who challenged conventional thinking, some of whom risked their lives in trying to reconstruct the past. To have the chance to get involved in such work was a dream coming true for him.

Another strand of his reading was Bible prophecy and its interpretation. He shared the belief, strongly held in some church circles, that Jesus is coming back soon, after a period of unparalleled troubles for the planet. It coloured his thinking and imbued him with a sense of urgency. "As it was in the days of Noah, so also will it be in the days of the Son of Man," the Lord had said. He sensed a hint there that his two great interests ran together in some way, that in the distant past might be found guidance for the immediate future.

Today Josiah and his friend Carl had met up for a mutual celebration. After weeks of waiting, Josiah had just received the offer to do gap year work for Seb Lowry. Wages would be low, but that did not dampen his excitement. For his part, Carl had just got his A-level results and confirmation of his place at University.

The pair eagerly discussed their hopes and plans. Carl preferred his definite study plans to Josiah's vaguer prospects.

Smiling slightly, a serious but friendly caution in his mind, he ribbed his friend. "How long do you think Seb Lowry's research will need?"

Josiah had to admit that he didn't know, but he insisted that the search for a lost civilization was worthwhile. He had many of the arguments from Ancient Quest and other books at his fingertips. "We know that the Sphinx, next to the Pyramids in Egypt, goes back almost to the last Ice Age, because it has rain weathering that's not consistent with more recent climate in Egypt. The pyramids don't show anything like the same weathering. We know of loads of megalithic structures around the world, with no easy explanation as to how primitive people could have built them. Some of those are so old that they're now under water – sea level has risen since they were built, as happened at the end of the Ice Age. We think that large parts of the world were mapped more accurately than should have been possible at the time. The circumstantial evidence demands that a lost civilization was behind all that. We just don't have the proof – yet."

"Some people say it was all done by aliens," said Carl.

Josiah wasn't sure if this was a serious comment or a jibe, but he gave a serious answer. "But we can't come up with a feasible plan to visit another solar system. The speed of light seems to be a speed limit, according to all that we know, so journeys would be impossibly long. And why would aliens want maps of places they never visit, and buildings that they never use? Why go to all that trouble and then leave it all behind?"

Carl couldn't think of an answer to that. "Who knows why aliens would do anything? Their motives might be... well, simply alien. Come to think of it, what if they had much longer lives than us? That would make the journey length much less of a problem. But more seriously, I've heard that some of these Atlantis hunters are New Agers and into some weird stuff. Are you sure that you can be involved in it, as a Christian?"

Josiah had considered this. "Sure, you have to be careful about that. But Lowry is definitely not a New Ager. He argues just as strongly against them as against conventional views, when he wants to. Take the hype over the Mayan calendar thing, a couple of years ago. In the ancient Mayan calendar, the Fifth Age of the world ran out just before Christmas 2012, and their traditions suggest that Ages end with disasters. The New Agers expected whole continents to move under our feet. Lowry simply said, the Mayans had a tradition of periodic disasters, and probably a good idea of the date of the last one. That gave them their Fifth Age start point in 3113 BC. Then they took three of their sacred numbers, multiplied them, and decided that the world would end in 360 x 260 x 20 days. It was just a guess, a nice round number in their terms."

"So you weren't surprised when the continents failed to shift under our feet?"

"No, I wasn't," said Josiah. "There were two theories advanced by the same researcher: one, that the world was mapped in antiquity; two, that the land masses periodically shift relative to the pole. The curious thing is, and I think Lowry was the first to point it out, the two theories contradict one another. The proof is that the analysis of the maps assumes the current world layout. Antarctica was mapped on polar coordinates, and the 80th parallel was confused with the Antarctic Circle. That could only happen if it was mapped in its current location."

Carl wanted to know more. "That 3113 BC date you mentioned earlier – is it at all reliable?"

"It might be." Josiah knew this topic well. His keen interest shone in his eyes. "It's very close to a date of similar significance in Indian tradition. Supposing something disastrous happened in 3113 BC, then maybe recovery might take three or four centuries, and that would account for various cultures seeming to have all emerged around 2800 or 2700 BC – Egypt, Mesopotamia, Indus Valley, China. And the Maya did have excellent information about the length of the year."

Carl recalled hearing something about that. "Were they the people who had a more accurate calendar than we have?"

"Again, some people put it that way, but it's misleading. Yes, their calendar was slightly better attuned to the right year length than ours is. Lowry points out that we could do better still, if we changed the traditions about leap years. All we'd have to do is decide that 4000 AD – I think that's the right year – should not be a leap year, and our calendar would gain an extra decimal place of accuracy, making it better than the Maya version. But that decision won't be taken for another nineteen hundred years.

"We aren't dealing with super men," continued Josiah. "Lowry makes that point time and again: they were just ordinary people with access to surprising knowledge. Lowry is after the truth of it. As Christians, we're after truth too. That's why I can work with him. If we both get our facts and our interpretations right, our truth and his truth can't contradict each other – truth can only complement truth."

Sport was Bethany's release. At University she had tried several of them. But her best role remained soccer midfield, using her stamina to chase up and down the pitch, and her rapport with her teammates to probe opposition defences. A male player of equivalent standard could have made a decent living for a few seasons with a professional club. In the women's game in Britain that still wasn't an option for more than a few, and Bethany was playing for fun.

She stood over a free kick, wondering what she might do with it. Right side of the field, level with the edge of the penalty box. One-all with less than ten minutes to play. At this early stage of the season, a first home win would set her team on course for a solid start. But they needed a goal. From straight in front of goal she might have tried a shot. The ground was firm and dry in the late summer sunshine, which was a help. But the angle to the goal was against her, the likelihood of sufficient power and accuracy slim. She decided to put in a cross. Enough balls into the penalty box was a bit like sticking a trowel in the ground enough times on a dig – sooner or later you got something.

Players from both teams jostled for position around the goalmouth. An underground train – above ground here on the outskirts of the city – rumbled past on the far side of the pitch. Bethany stepped back to take a run at the ball.

"Go Fisher!" came a raucous cry. Bethany looked round and saw a striking young blonde woman waving a hand and shouting encouragement. It wasn't one of the small number of regular fans; Bethany didn't recognise her. She shook her head at the attention seeking, collected her thoughts, and chipped the ball into the area. A header turned it goalwards. A flurry of legs tried to hasten it onward or sweep it away. One of the forwards ended the skirmish by driving the ball home. Two-one.

That remained the final score. By the time Bethany and her teammates emerged from the small and ill-maintained clubhouse to go and celebrate the win, all but their closest friends among the fans had dispersed homewards. Except for the loud blonde, still there, standing alone, a stranger to the crowd as well as to the players. She was still after Bethany's attention.

"Great free kick," she remarked as Bethany passed her.

The midfielder knew the goal had little to do with her. "Pretty average, really," she commented dryly, not keen on the misplaced enthusiasm.

"Modest too," came the reply, "but Seb says you're something special."

Bethany sighed. Seb? She looked at the stranger with an irritated question in her eyes.

"I'm his partner, Helen – Helen Carr. Pleased to meet you."

Bethany regarded Helen disdainfully for a few seconds, hoping to think of a polite way to brush her off. "We're just heading off for a post-match team drink," she tried.

"Fine," came the reply, "I'll buy."

Bethany grimaced, but felt compelled to let the woman tag along.

To Bethany's relief, Helen wasn't there to talk shop. In fact the details of Seb's work appeared to bore her, but the travel opportunities were a different matter. She talked animatedly of the bird and animal life she'd encountered in the vicinity of research in South America, Africa and Asia. "I've seen penguins in the tropics," was one example, "while Seb was examining pyramids in Peru. There's some current that they get caught in and swept away from the Antarctic. And the same current supplies cold water a long way up the South American coast, so the water isn't too hot for them."

As the conversation continued, a picture emerged of an unusual sort of relationship, which happened to work for the two people concerned. Helen wanted an exotic and nomadic life; Seb wanted an attractive younger woman. The latter didn't surprise Bethany; in fact the thought had been nagging at her whenever her lack of other job offers brought Seb's back to her mind. But it seemed he already had one in tow – and Bethany made it clear that she had no plans to try to change that. If Seb, Helen and Bethany were all content with the status quo in that respect, maybe this was one doubt resolved.

Two figures emerged from a corner of the pub. "Hi Bethany," said the smaller one.

She recognised Carl, and then Josiah behind him. "Here's the guy that was pestering your boyfriend while he was trying to pester me," she explained to Helen.

"Josiah," said Helen in surprise. She'd heard Seb mention the name. "We'll be seeing more of each other while you're working for Seb." She introduced herself.

"I didn't know Seb had a partner," said Josiah. "Pleased to meet you." He was somewhat abashed by her attractiveness, and had to remind himself that she was already attached.

Helen smiled. "We'll be meeting again soon. You know your parents have invited Seb over, to fill them in on what you'll be doing. I'm tagging along to the get-together."

3

The Puzzle Outlined

Seb and Helen were back in London, to meet with Josiah's family and discuss what his gap year work might involve. The Hopes were used to entertaining for church functions, and their well-practised hospitality soon made a good impression on the visitors. After dinner, they adjourned to the comfortable sitting room, which was well-furnished and often used for house group meetings.

Mr and Mrs Hope ushered Seb and Helen to one sofa, and seated themselves on the other, facing them. The respectable, comfortably off couple, through their silver wedding anniversary and still going strong, made quite a contrast with the adventurer and his ex-model live-in girlfriend. Seb was approaching forty, his skin somewhat darkened and dried by long travelling in hot climates, but still a pretty fit guy. Bethany, had she known of it, would have approved of his fitness regime at least. Helen, slightly more than ten years his junior, had more obvious assets, which were as much on display as she figured would be seemly in a religious household. She might have reassured herself that Bethany wasn't chasing her man, but she wasn't sure of the reverse. And she couldn't match Bethany on youth or intelligence. Was she in danger of being dumped? Not without a fight, if it proved necessary, that was for sure.

Josiah sat beside a small table by the other wall, opposite his elder brother Paul, who had remained somewhat aloof over dinner and was now studying a position on a chessboard. Between the Hopes and the window, to Seb's surprise and delight, sat Bethany Fisher. Mrs Hope had persuaded her to come along, as a way of getting independent informed comment on Seb's views. Bethany was currently figuring how much extra training would be needed to counter the effects of the Hopes' delicious meal, while hoping she would not come under more pressure from Lowry.

Josiah was keen to get the conversation on to business. "So, how is the sequel to Ancient Quest going?" he asked.

Seb started to talk enthusiastically. "You already know I was recently in Malta, where I found the map that had belonged to the Turkish would-be conqueror, Admiral Piali. I'll come back to the map later. On my way home, I stopped off in the Italian Tyrol to have a look round the Bolzano Archaeological Museum, where the Iceman's body is preserved."

Josiah's parents were already looking blank. Seb hastened to add in more detail. "Just over twenty years ago, a five thousand year old body was found, preserved in the ice near the border between Italy and Austria. They call him the Iceman, or sometimes Otzi after the name of the glacier in which he was lying. The guy had a lot of equipment with him, including a copper axe." He couldn't resist a quip. "Copper in the Stone Age. That's one of the anomalies which Bethany's been taught to ignore."

Bethany glared, appreciating neither the joke nor the possibility of a confrontation. She was hoping for a quiet evening. Trying to control her annoyance, she broke in. "Archaeology hasn't failed just because there's no answer yet. Anyway the Iceman's age is exaggerated. The 5300 year figure is the maximum, to attract tourists – the older the better. The low end of the radiocarbon dating range is two or three centuries later." Seb shrugged, dismissing that as insignificant, but Bethany continued. "Then there are calibration issues. We know, for instance, that many Egyptian calibrated radiocarbon dates are too high to fit the history. The radiocarbon dates were calibrated by use of tree ring sequences, but the calibration method has been severely questioned. If the date for the Iceman is a calibrated one, that could knock around another ten per cent – about five hundred years – off his real age as indicated by the raw data. And you don't need a lost civilization to explain copper in 2500 BC."

Realizing that sounded too combative, she hurriedly threw in an anecdote to defuse things. "I went to that museum myself, on a school holiday trip to the Alps. I listened to all the commentaries twice, looked into every corner, every exhibit. The rest of the group were keen to get back to skiing and went on ahead. They had lunch before noticing I was missing. One of the teachers had to come back and drag me out."

It was clear that Seb approved of such enthusiasm for his pet subject. Helen jabbed him sharply. "Aren't you glad I can't knock your arguments down like that?" Seb nodded behind a grimace. Reassured, Helen tried a further comment. She'd hung around Seb long enough to pick up odds and ends, enough to be sure she wouldn't look stupid. "How can something scientific like radiocarbon dating be that many hundreds of years out?"

To Bethany's surprise, it was Josiah who jumped in on the point. "There are certain unprovable assumptions involved, like how much Carbon-14 – that's the radioactive type – was around so long ago. Scientists assume it was the same proportion as today, but they could be wrong. I've read some surprising critiques in..." He decided to leave out the word 'creationist'. "...some articles. Radiocarbon dating is only good for the last fifty thousand years, but one time people managed to get a measurable radiocarbon date out of some wood found in rock from before the time of the dinosaurs. Something about the method is less than fool-proof."

Bethany wasn't happy about that line of discussion. "I'm only talking about a ten per cent discrepancy, that could easily be natural variation in Carbon-14 levels. To take a concrete example, did you see that TV programme on the plagues of Egypt a couple of weeks back?" There were nods around the room; biblical ancient history was a common interest for most of those present. "Right, well, the Bible puts the plagues and the Exodus at around 1450 BC. It used to be thought that a massive eruption on the Mediterranean island of Thera happened at around the same time. So – just like that programme did – people have tried to explain the plagues as natural consequences of the eruption. But when what's called the New or Revised Chronology for Egypt came along in the 1990s, it confirmed the Exodus date but put the Thera eruption nearly three hundred years forward, 1200 BC or earlier. We know which Egyptian dynasty was reigning when the eruption occurred. The radiocarbon gurus still want the eruption to have been around 1500 or even 1600 BC, but the history just won't fit that way."

Although impressed by Bethany's knowledge, Seb had an objection. "I didn't realise that the New Chronology had been generally accepted."

She was quick to respond. "It's still controversial. Scholars who don't like to admit a historical basis to the Bible have a vested interest in fighting it. But it's gaining more credibility year by year. I'm definitely on that side of the argument."

Seb nodded. "I admit I don't share your religion. But even if I think that the Bible is just folk tales, I wouldn't dismiss it as a source of information."

Josiah's parents were looking uncomfortable with that remark. Bethany noticed and turned to them, trying to offer reassurance. "It's like I might be prepared to accept that there could be authentic memories preserved in the Koran, as well as in the Bible. That wouldn't make me a Muslim. I've tried telling Mr Lowry that he doesn't know what he's missing by rejecting Jesus. For a non-believer, it's a fair and honest attitude, and I've worked with other people who think like that."

Seb resumed his tale. "And remember what the likes of Heyerdahl and Severin achieved by listening to folk tales. But to continue with my travels, I was really startled to find a menhir – a standing stone – in that Bolzano museum. I thought that they were confined to the Atlantic coasts and Malta, but it seems that Italy had them as well. This one has a carving, showing a man with an axe just like the Iceman's. That seems to relate the Iceman to the time of the European megalithic monuments, which predate the pyramids." Suddenly a possible objection occurred to him, and he looked towards Bethany. "Or have you revised that dating?"

It was Bethany's turn to smile. "If you shift all the Carbon-14 dates ten per cent, or whatever, the older ones are still older than the earlier ones, it's just that they're a bit closer together. Carry on."

"Well, then I had another stroke of fortune. A handful of 'proper researchers' aren't afraid to be seen with me. One of them happened to be on a dig in the nearby spa town of Merano, and he showed me some very interesting remains."

Paul stopped studying his chess pieces and looked up. "Massacre in Merano," he said.

Seb gaped. "You know about this?"

"Sure," said Paul. "The 1981 World Chess Championship match. Anatoly Karpov beat Viktor Korchnoi by 6 wins to 2, with 10 draws – a quick match. Their previous match, in 1978, Karpov won 6 to 5 after 35 games in all. That one's known as The Battle of Baguio City. Excuse me, I'm due to play a game on the Internet." He rose and left the room.

Seb stared after him. His mum tried to explain. "Paul has Asperger Syndrome – a mild sort of autism. He's one of London's top chess players, but has a trouble with social behaviour. He just picked up on your mentioning the town name and overlooked the rest of what you were saying. He wants to be friendly, but can be rude without realizing it."

Seb nodded his acceptance of the explanation. He wanted to keep on the subject. "To return to my point, there was a massacre in Merano, but not last century. It's just come to light last year while some agricultural land was being redeveloped for tourism. A number of bodies, violently killed, were found in and around an ancient homestead. Radiocarbon dating puts them roughly contemporary with the Iceman, maybe a few decades older, but the ranges overlap quite a bit. A broken piece of bronze was sticking out of a bone. So, Bethany, what do you say to bronze in the Stone Age?"

"If it's contemporary with the Iceman, that makes it later than the Stone Age," snapped Bethany, annoyed at the goad. "But bronze that early is out of the question. There has to be some contamination or other error on the radiocarbon date."

Seb smiled in mock approval. "The obvious conventional explanation. Very convenient. There was also an axe handle with some decoration." He produced a tracing from a folder in his briefcase. "A circle, and a vertical line either side. I think it denotes a sun symbol and taking an alignment between two standing stones or sticks." He handed the tracing round. Bethany had no contrary interpretation to offer. "That's a clue for another time. I can't figure any significance to it yet. Meanwhile, we have the map I showed you before. A marginal note linked to Malta has a sort of riddle which I've had translated." He found the relevant sheet of paper and recited.

"The children of Zeus vanquished Atlas,
when the sky fell to earth.
The sea swallowed its princes,
the Guardian from the mountains abides.
The people were scattered,
but their wisdom was gathered.
Hidden from the eye of Osiris
are the secret Treasures of Zeus.
When heaven chooses to reveal the way,
slay Osiris and enter."

Bethany looked blank, but Josiah recalled something he'd read. "Didn't you say in Ancient Quest that 'the sky falling to earth' was a description used of the disaster that destroyed an ancient civilization?"

Seb nodded and continued, "And this specifically refers to Atlas, who gave his name to Atlantis. The princes of the sea, who were swallowed, should indicate Atlantis as well. You can understand the survivors being scattered.

"Also, the eye of Horus or Osiris is a frequent motif on Malta. That would be why Piali associated the riddle with Malta. Something is hidden there; the gathered wisdom of the scattered people, the Treasures of Zeus – I think they both refer to the same thing."

"And the Guardian?" asked Josiah.

"So far, I've no idea. But I think it's significant that he's described as being from the mountains. The low-lying land was devastated by the sea, but the mountains were safe as a refuge. But this is my target, the thing I want Josiah to help me find. Bethany too, if you like."

She shook her head firmly.

"I have a number of preparations to make and commitments to fulfil first. Besides, I don't like the heat of the Mediterranean summer. The worst thing about these ancient clues is that they all seem to be in hot countries. I reckon to go out to Malta and start searching around the beginning of November. The daytime temperature should be no more than around twenty degrees then. The only problem is the shorter number of daylight hours. I'd prefer to go in spring, when there's more daylight but it's still not too hot, except that I don't fancy the longer delay."

The conversation went on, to no great purpose. Josiah's parents were forming a generally favourable impression of their son's potential employer. Bethany was struggling to suppress the desire to help chase down Seb Lowry's clues. Ancient mysteries were a passion for her too; she had to keep reminding herself of the damage to her prospects that being associated with him would cause.

Meanwhile, upstairs, Paul was in a deep strategic battle over a virtual chessboard. While waiting for his opponent to move, he tried to relax by logging on to an Internet chat forum. Several of his online contacts were already chatting. Soon he was telling them about Seb Lowry's visit.

On the other side of the country, a moderator of the forum ran a finger down a list of topics that were of interest to friends of his. He found Seb Lowry's name on the list, and immediately started quizzing Paul about him. It was natural for Paul to be open and unguarded, and soon he was relating Seb's interest in the 'Treasures of Zeus', little realising that this was information that Seb would not want widely known. Fortunately he had not heard all the talk downstairs, indeed he only knew the phrase 'Treasures of Zeus' from his brother's earlier meeting at the church. But it was enough for his supposed friend to be jotting down notes, and then sending the information on, in anticipation of a small reward.

4

Plans

Vic Osgood followed his new boss into the plush inner sanctum of a top London club. The ambitious young researcher had always had an eye for the right contacts, the ones with fingers on the hidden levers of power. His quick mind and – how should one put it? – *flexibility* in matters of principle had both helped to get him noticed in such circles. It was not many weeks since word had been passed to him that the eminent Professor Mannis needed a new assistant. At first, he had not understood why his friends should want to place him alongside an ivory tower historian. But now, following in Mannis's footsteps into some secret and powerful gathering, he was beginning to feel like a jackpot winner. Clearly, the professor had more influence than one might think. Whom was he about to meet, and how far up the ladder could they boost him?

The committee would have seemed a strange mixture to anyone unaware of the common bond between them. A senior liberal theologian sat alongside an official of a leading humanist group. A top industrialist, stalwart of the Britain in Europe campaign, was there. So was a young junior minister, a rising star of government, who was conversing freely with a high-ranking civil servant from the Foreign Office. Also present was a pop promoter, someone who was helping to mould the tastes, fashions and opinions of the rising generation.

Osgood was introduced to each of them in turn. He heard Mannis explain that his job would be fieldwork in an important project.

"I'm getting a little too old to do all of it myself. So we need to initiate young Vic here into what's at stake."

The humanist official took up the tale. "The problem is Seb Lowry." Several eyebrows were raised. Most of those present knew of Lowry, but not as a person of any significance. Had something changed? "Yes, the matchstick civilization man. Unfortunately, he's somehow stumbled on to something important. You know how we got one of our people on to the list of contacts that Lowry e-mails when he thinks he's found a lead and is looking for further information. Well, the latest news is, Lowry has got a lead on the Treasures of Zeus."

The more highly initiated members of the group gasped. Osgood looked blank.

"Vic needs to understand this more," put in Mannis.

"Ah, yes." The humanist turned to Osgood. "According to some of our most secret traditions, the original Zeus – you can forget the later mythology – was the ruler of Athens and a chief opponent of Osiris. You know who Osiris was, of course?"

Vic hoped that his limited knowledge – a mixture of history and esoteric tradition – would be enough to avoid embarrassment. "He was the great benefactor and leader of the first world government and, through his son Horus, the founder of the dynasties of Egypt. Synonymous with Orion, whom the Egyptians worshipped. Also known as On."

"That's right. Now, our secret records tell how this would-be world leader was bitterly opposed by a man known simply as the Man of Division. This man sent out envoys, who succeeded in seizing power in certain key locations, such as Zeus in Athens and Seth in the Nile Delta. Their resistance is reflected in the myths, as when Seth supposedly killed Osiris and was later himself slain by the avenging son Horus.

"The point is simply this. Our goal is ultimately to re-establish Osiris' harmonious kingdom, the golden age that the Egyptians looked back to. One political structure, one economy, one religion. The various moves towards regional unity in recent decades – political and monetary unions, and so forth – are just the first step. We don't know what the 'Treasures of Zeus' might be, but we can infer that they are propaganda from the other side, from a key aide of the Man of Division. We do not want Lowry presenting that to the world."

Not everyone was convinced. The junior minister spoke for them. "But no matter what he finds, at the end of the day, Lowry is only another crank theoriser. Surely it's only the small minority of cranks who will pay serious attention? What do they matter?"

It was the theologian who replied. "I wish it were that simple. The surprising difficulty in bringing about religious unity is that the most passionately religious people – the fundamentalists – are the most opposed to it. They all believe in their own exclusive truth, you see. Supposing Lowry came up with something which they thought supported their case, they would grab hold of it and could do a significant amount of damage. There are still over a million Christian fundamentalists in this country, not counting the Jewish and Muslim varieties, and millions more across the States and in some Commonwealth countries. It would be foolish to underestimate them."

"Couldn't we just have Lowry bumped off?" came the next question. "Wouldn't his knowledge die with him?"

Mannis shook his head. "We don't know for sure who his confidants are. So far, all Lowry has is a few clues that he thinks may lead him somewhere. But if people with clues start disappearing, our experience is that conspiracy theorists start to sniff out why. Better to let him search, just make sure that he doesn't find anything that he can make use of."

Osgood was puzzled. "I don't see what you want me to do."

"We will be watching Lowry, finding out what his plans are and where he's going. If it looks like he's found a significant location, you'll be sent there first. Then you can make sure that there's nothing there for him to find."

"How do we know that he will tell us where he's going?" asked Osgood.

The professor smiled. "We've got another source of information. I have people who monitor Internet forums for us, checking on selected topics; one of them reports that Lowry has signed up an assistant, a gap-year student named Josiah Hope. The information was volunteered unknowingly by Josiah's brother.

"We found out that the Hope family go to a church in north London. I'll be getting one of our people to go along to that church and make contact with the brother. He has Asperger Syndrome; he's likely to be quite naïve about activities such as ours, and open about what's going on to anyone who shows an interest. He'll pass on whatever his brother tells him about Lowry's plans."

"You're telling someone to go to church?" Osgood was amused.

"Yes," said Mannis. "Nasty work, but someone has to do it." A ripple of laughter went round the room.

"Lucky you had someone on that forum," commented Osgood.

Several pairs of eyes rolled. Osgood's neighbour leaned over to him. "You understand political correctness, yes – how we tell people what is okay to think?" Osgood nodded. "Well, we have to be careful of people who see the world differently. Judaeo-Christians mainly, yes, but others too. Most people are anxious to fit in as best they can, but occasionally you get one who's prepared to go out on a limb with their own ideas. That's why we had to try to make an example of that hacker who was after evidence of aliens. We don't mind people hunting aliens, but what if someone got a similar obsession about stuff that did affect us? So we watch a lot of online forums closely, just in case."

"We have eyes and ears in a lot of places," added Mannis. "Anyone who shows signs of independent thought can be a potential obstacle. We don't have a lot of naked power to wield; we prefer to influence hearts and minds so that people bend to our will without realising it. It's not 100% successful in every case in the short term, but it keeps on gaining us ground."

Bethany stood at a window, looking out over a landscaped lawn towards a tree-lined stream. Through the gaps in the trees she could see miles of rolling English countryside. On the lawn, other participants in her church's young adults retreat were sitting, chatting, laughing together. The scene was lovely. But its very happiness, the serenity of all the others, seemed only to emphasize the uncertainties in her own life. She was in debt from her studies, unemployed, unable to see the next step ahead. She was there hoping to do business with God, to find some answers, but nothing was happening. Yes, God was there, she had no doubt of that; it was just that he didn't seem to be in any hurry to deal with her job problem.

She thought back to her early teenage years. A new believer coming under pressure from her peers and teachers to give a sensible reason for having faith. A television series – an old one, repeated on cable – that had questioned the entire historical basis of the Old Testament. "You believe in nothing more than myths," she had been told. Going in distress to a church youth leader, then getting a visit a few days later from a deacon. He'd brought a book for her. It went through the same archaeological data as the television series, but reinterpreted the timeline, finding evidence for the real existence of Solomon, David, Saul, Joseph, and the whole Exodus and conquest story. The key, it seemed, was to get the dating right.

Bethany had read through the large book in a matter of days; finding her doubts dispelled, learning anew that the Bible could be trusted after all. In that short time a dream had formed in her heart. She wanted to be part of the process, to make discoveries that would plug the gaps that still loomed between conventional thought and the Bible record. She had always believed that God had put that dream in her heart, that he had dreamed it for her. But now the doubts were beginning to crowd in again.

Suddenly she was conscious of Kath, her younger sister and roommate for the weekend, close beside her. "Finding waiting on the Lord trying?" queried Kath gently.

Bethany threw up her hands in frustration, and tried to articulate her mood. "I'm just so confused and frustrated. It's like God's there but he isn't quite there for me, or like he cares so much about everything except what I need. I want to follow him but I don't know which way he's leading. I'm getting general assurances of love, when I need specifics."

Kath was longing to give reassurance. She reminded Bethany of Christian friends who had also had long waits for jobs. "And you have got this volunteer work on the hill forts project coming up."

Bethany nodded. "It's better than nothing at all, but it's not paid. The first assignment is western Cornwall. I'll be able to stay at the guesthouse we used on our family trip there, so that's good. And I'm not going within five miles of Zennor."

Kath reddened. Even though she'd been only a kid then, only very recently saved, it had been a stupid thing to blurt out, standing by the carving in the Cornish village church. It still embarrassed her to recall it. "I get this sense that God is going to use you to find the truth behind the mermaid story," she had said. It was part of the family folklore now, probably being saved for a wedding day speech along with other embarrassments like... She decided not to pursue that line of thought.

Instead Kath returned to Bethany's situation, re-checking how her job applications were going, citing Bible verses about God's promises to his people. But the facts, true though she knew them to be, were not getting through to Bethany's emotions. Kath decided to try another tack. "Maybe your mind is closed to the thing he wants you to look at. You know in your head that you can trust his leading. Just the once, ask him, should you be going to look for Atlantis? You never know, you might get a clear 'NO!'"

Bethany seized the opportunity to vent her emotions. The objections came thick and fast: poor pay, no long-term job security, damage to career prospects, and the lingering suspicion – not completely resolved by her chat with Helen – that Seb Lowry wanted a pretty assistant to seduce.

Kath nodded to show that she understood them all, but responded, "It sounds to me like Helen expects to be on the trip.

You can make sure of that before you sign up. If she wants Seb as a lover and you don't, Seb will see where his best interests lie even if he's not sure at the moment. And Josiah says that Seb does like to cultivate professional contacts – male and female – there's a good chance that you're just one more on that list. As for the other objections, they're not overriding objections in God's eyes, are they? I know how much you've dreamt of making some spectacular discovery. Maybe God put that dream in your heart, and maybe this is his way of fulfilling it. You lose nothing by asking."

Bethany pondered. At last she sighed and sank into a chair, lowering her eyes. Her voice was muted by doubts, but honest. "OK, Lord, if you really want me to work with Lowry, I'm listening. Tell me if you must."

She put her hands over her ears. It was one of their pet jokes and they both laughed – it was no way to stop God speaking. But for the moment there was still no answer. Bethany found herself hoping that the absence of a yes was an implicit no.

5

Valley of the Iceman

T he car sped north along one of the motorways out of Verona. At the wheel was Seb's Tyrolean contact, the man who had shown him the decorated axe handle, Christian Strauss. Beside him sat Josiah, on his first visit to Italy, eagerly anticipating what lay ahead. Behind them, Seb and Helen had chosen to sit together in the back.

Both in name and appearance, Christian was clearly German. An archaeologist in his forties, fair hair cut short, bright eyes that one could imagine peering through the mists of time. Josiah asked how long he'd been in Italy, and was surprised to learn that Christian was a native. "This used to be Austrian land, until the end of the Great War in 1918. There are still more German speakers than Italian speakers in this province."

"Makes it difficult for us Brits," put in Helen, who had visited the area on holiday a few years earlier. "You can't rely on people knowing English as their second language round here. They all have to learn German and Italian first."

The long, narrow and almost straight valley ran slightly east of due north for fully seventy-five miles, starting just above Verona. A river meandered back and forth along its length, criss-crossing road and railway frequently. On both sides the land rose in steep and often wooded slopes, four thousand feet and more, towering above them and seldom, it seemed, more than a mile from the road. Some of the slopes held seemingly inaccessible castles, which once commanded access to the upper parts of the valley.

"You can see there the traces of the glacier action which cut this valley," remarked Christian, pointing out an exposed rock face. Josiah looked, said nothing; but inwardly he grinned. It was not three months since he'd been to a presentation of a DVD on the Mount St Helen's eruption of 1980. In the thirty plus years since then, data from the eruption had challenged a number of theories. Josiah remembered seeing a canyon, cut in a single day by a massive mudflow, yet looking exactly like others which geologists thought were formed slowly over vast eons. He could easily imagine waters draining off the Alpine heights as the great Flood receded, carving this great scar through freshly raised hills in a very short space of time.

Beyond Bolzano, where the body of the Iceman lies in the purpose-built Archaeological Museum, the valley bent back westward of due north. Here it was the valley of the river Etsch, but ahead of them it joined with the valleys of the Passer and Vinschgau, the latter where the Iceman had started his fateful climb to death on an Alpine pass. At that junction lay their destination, the spa town of Merano. Here Seb was going to show Josiah the finds which he'd described while at his family home, barely two weeks before.

It was evening when they arrived, so work was deferred to the following day. In the morning Seb and Helen showed Josiah the promenades either side of the Passer river, which cascaded foaming through the centre of the town. Beside the river they paused for a snack, admiring the floral displays along the route. Josiah remembered to take one particular photo to show his brother: the Kursaal by the river, venue for the 1981 world chess championship match. The area was not particularly crowded; the summer tourist season was coming to an end. Although it was only mid-September, soon the Dolomites would be too cold for summer walkers. Winter skiers would replace them, but not for some weeks.

Northward from the river, they passed a shopping arcade. "I had the best baguette I've ever tasted down there," remarked Helen, "accompanied by a totally ghastly lemon sparkling mineral water. The waitress and I spoke four languages between us, and none of them were common to both of us."

They moved on northwestward towards Christian's dig site. A new tourist facility was planned on the site of a former apple orchard near the railway, and the archaeologist had been allowed a brief window of opportunity for field work. He was at the gate to greet them. "Welcome to our look into Merano's past," he started enthusiastically. "No one knew how far back in history this place went, until now. We just had a general idea that it was settled in pre-Roman times. But this, this is as old as what you see at the Bolzano museum, five thousand years and more." He pointed out the unearthed remains of a homestead, probably the centre of a small farm. "This was the fireplace; here we found ash for carbon dating."

Josiah felt that he ought to say something to show interest. "Would this area have been settled because it's good farming land?"

Christian was quick to agree. "Good soil, still today used for growing apples. Good water supply from the rivers. Good trade routes along the valleys. And good defence, guarded by the rivers and with the hills to retreat to." He gestured eastwards to the low ridge where sat the village of Dorf Tirol. Though high above the town, it was in turn overshadowed by the mountains to the north, while other peaks showed close by, both eastward and westward.

An assistant dashed up and whispered something in Christian's ear. Christian looked both surprised and apologetic. "Excuse me," he said. "I am told we have another distinguished visitor to our site. Please wait here." He left hurriedly.

Seb bent down and examined the stones that marked where walls had once stood. Helen, feeling a bit left out, seized the moment to enter the conversation. "The mountains to the east are the Dolomites," she told Josiah. "You get into them by narrow roads with fantastic series of hairpin bends. I went up there several years ago, before I met Seb. The coach driver was very skilful and confident, otherwise I would have been scared of coming off the road and tumbling down the slopes. There are some lovely views up there, but you need to come in high summer to have a decent chance of good weather. This time of year you could easily get caught in a chilly afternoon storm."

She was interrupted by Christian's return. He was not alone. "Mr Lowry, may I present to you the great English archaeologist, Hugh Mannis, and his assistant, Mr Osgood. Professor, this is your country's adventurer and writer, Sebastian Lowry."

Lowry and Mannis regarded each other coldly. Their paths had crossed before, and neither liked the other. Mannis was in any case aloof, sharp, hard to get on with unless you were in his circle. He made no effort to hide his disdain for those who trespassed on his turf without the appropriate qualifications. Seb, for his part, saw Mannis as an establishment figure, too wedded to conventional thinking to entertain the more imaginative leaps which might explain mysteries. Neither offered to shake hands.

Christian tried to break the ice between them. "Professor, this is Mr Lowry's assistant, Josiah Hope, and his partner, Helen Carr."

Mannis glanced at them. Helen he knew by sight and repute, Josiah was obviously too young to be qualified. "Amateurs," he growled. "Be sure not to touch anything. When are you going to find qualified help, Lowry? Or are you scared you'd be out of your depth with it?"

"Actually I'm saving my expert help," said Seb. "For a shock tactic, you know." For a couple of seconds he held his powerful forearms horizontally, pointing out in front of him, trying to imitate the front paws of the sphinx. Osgood suppressed a snigger.

Mannis ignored the attempt at humour. If indeed he recognised it. He turned back to Christian. "Where is that carved axe handle – if you please?"

"Ah, yes. Mr Lowry has already seen that. Why don't you all come this way?" Christian led the way to his site office. The axe lay prominently on his desk. Mannis snatched it up at once; it was his way of asserting priority over the amateurs around him. He showed the carving to his assistant, and muttered something that no one else heard. Seb saw Osgood react, and wondered what the cue had been.

Christian eyed the two of them as they examined the axe. Mannis was reluctant to hand it back, but he could hardly keep hold of it for ever. He turned it over and over, pondering what would come across as a persuasive opinion. Finally he found his voice. "Late intrusion, or maybe your dating is suspect," he asserted. "I've seen the lines and circle motif before; it's first millennium BC at the earliest."

Christian was shocked, but determined to defend his work. He referred to the site stratigraphy, and fished out his notes to confirm exactly where it had been found.

Mannis jumped on a mention of a nearby piece of bronze. "That confirms it, the date cannot be anywhere near as early as you're suggesting."

Christian handed the axe to Seb, who showed it to Josiah. Helen peered round their shoulders, trying to show an interest. Christian was hoping for support. It wasn't forthcoming.

"What this professor is saying agrees with what Bethany said, when you described this find," pointed out Josiah.

Seb grunted, irritated. "But it doesn't agree with Christian's field work," he snapped.

Josiah was not deterred. "Remember what Bethany and I said about carbon dating before, at my place. I'm not sure you can trust it," he ventured.

"Show me something better to use instead," was Seb's reasonable but sharp riposte.

Josiah knew what a creationist would say: question the unprovable assumptions, trust the timeline in the Bible and work from that as a more reliable basis. He knew that would not go down well with anyone else in the room, so chose to hold his tongue.

Helen broke the ensuing silence. "It reminds me of the Japanese flag," she said, referring to the carving. "You know, the rising sun." Mannis almost made a comment, but thought better of it.

"Yes," said Seb, "that's what I've said all along; it's a sunrise or sunset and an alignment with standing stones. And that way of observing the heavens is ancient – three or four thousand years BC at least."

Christian smiled as his viewpoint was at last bolstered, though he was far too cautious to buy Seb's line as anything more than speculation.

Mannis glowered. "There's nothing of interest here," he muttered to his assistant. The pair of them stomped off.

Josiah laid the axe back on the desk.

Seb seemed lost in thought. "He knows something, I can feel it. He's trying to put me off the scent. Has he really seen the motif before, and if so, where? I've never seen anything like it." His musings ran out of steam and stopped.

Helen had a question. "Why did you do that sign with your forearms?" Seb had forgotten what she was talking about. "When you said you were saving your expert help," she prompted. Still there was no response. "Something about shock tactics?"

That word triggered the memory. "Oh yes, shock. There was a geologist named Schoch, who authenticated the theory that the Sphinx at Giza is older than the pyramids. It gave a lot of credence to some of my fellow maverick theorists. Irritated Mannis and his friends no end, at the time. I was trying to look like a sphinx as I said it – arms extended like the front paws."

6

Cornwall

Seb Lowry had walked up to the old hilltop earthwork fort in the afternoon. He liked the country air; besides, the one downside to having Helen with him was that having no interest in the archaeology itself, she liked to grab the car for sightseeing trips. He'd found it best to concede the point today. It had been a stiffish climb; he was relieved to find that the last phase levelled out, indeed it was the only reasonable way to the top. Approaching the heart of the fort, he saw digging in progress as he'd been told. A large project to map hill fort sites across Britain was under way, and this was one of the first sites to be investigated. One of the team looked up. Seb was recognised, though not particularly welcome here.

"Mr Lowry," came a cool greeting, "I'm sorry but we haven't dug up Atlantis for you today."

Seb was used to this. Although he had valued contacts in archaeological circles, the majority were resentful of his maverick approach. "Well," he replied, "I understand Atlantis is the alleged first civilization west of the Pillars of Hercules. And the Cornish megaliths round here represent part of the first known culture on the northeastern Atlantic coasts. Are you really sure that they're not one and the same?" The only answer was a derisive chuckle.

Seb wandered around eyeing the site. Various spots were being meticulously examined. The whole site was plotted on a grid; some of the work was at selected grid points by particularly interesting stones, other work was at seemingly random intervals. The hilltop was fairly flat, with grassy footpaths between heaps of stones and the more overgrown areas; enough space to walk about, but on every side except the one he'd approached by, steep gorse-covered slopes remained formidable defences. No one was keen to talk to him. Then he spotted another visitor, who was being treated much more respectfully. No surprise to see the eminent Professor Mannis get such treatment. Was this an odd coincidence, running across Mannis again so soon, or were they both sniffing around the same trail without realising it?

Seb edged closer to the conversation. "...three copper pieces. Or possibly two. These might fit together so." As the site worker demonstrated the fit, Lowry saw Mannis start. He edged even nearer. Mannis was speaking. "Er... my new assistant – you'll have to meet him sometime – a very promising research student named Osgood – he specialises in early metal artefacts such as copper. But he's too busy to drag down here at present. I'd really like to be allowed to borrow these for his inspection for a day or two, bring you back an expert analysis." Something in his voice rang false.

Seb stepped into the conversation. "Hello... I wasn't expecting you here," he remarked.

Mannis sneered. "Expert help is always welcome. As you would know, if you had any to offer."

Seb tried to ignore the barb. "So what have you found?" He wasn't sure if he'd get an answer. But even Mannis could hardly deny the existence of something that was right there in his hand.

"Just some copper relics. Not even on the site, exactly, but down at the bottom of the eastern slope. Probably not significant."

It was obvious both that Mannis was downplaying something important and that Seb was not wanted. He excused himself and walked to the eastern edge of the fort. It wasn't easy to find the only reasonably practical track down, and while looking for it he had time to appreciate the view. Southwards lay Mount Bay and St Michael's Mount, northeast was the Hayle estuary. This single vantage point commanded the entire isthmus before the last tip of Cornwall. The strategic value of the fort was clear.

Carefully Seb descended the steep slope, then, still dodging between bushes at every step, worked his way left towards two volunteer diggers he'd spotted from above. In the late September heat – increasingly common in Britain in recent years – they were taking a short break. One of the voices sounded slightly familiar. "Come to dinner on Thursday. This is where I'm staying," he heard. A flier was fumbled and dropped to the floor. Seb bent to retrieve it, and instinctively noted a name as he handed it back to the owner. As he rose, each recognised the other. Surprise was mutual.

"This is Seb Lowry – the lost civilization hunter," said Bethany Fisher to her colleague. Then to Seb, with deep suspicion, "What are you doing here?"

Seb managed to reassure Bethany that their meeting was simply coincidence. He had come with no idea that she was there. Having managed this, he persuaded her more easily to compare notes. It was indeed Bethany who, that very morning, had unearthed three old and rusty copper fragments. She had merely documented the location and passed them to the site director. Her normal enthusiasm was severely dampened by this assignment on the less important perimeter of the fort, even though she knew it was a random choice and someone had to do it. But she agreed with Seb's suspicions about Mannis borrowing the fragments. "If I were the expert, and if they were important, I'd want to come here and see the context."

Seb pulled out his mobile phone and started making calls; firstly a cab to speed him back to town, then a summons to his partner. Helen's fury at being called away from seal watching was plain, but she knew better than to interfere with Seb's passion for his research. Grudgingly, she agreed to meet up. Seb asked Bethany to come with him, but she was forced to refuse. Even if she'd wanted to go, she was committed to work.

Seb simply asked the cab to take him to the best hotel in St Ives. He was not surprised to find Mannis's expensive Mercedes parked outside. Taking a restaurant seat from where the said car was in clear view, he tried to improve Helen's mood by treating her to an expensive dinner.

Mannis walked into the restaurant and Seb's ambush. "What should I tell my readers about your copper relics?" came the question.

"Nothing," was the snappy response. Mannis turned and retreated to his room, totally unwilling to discuss anything. This was looking decidedly odd, reflected Seb.

Thirty minutes later, dinner was over and Mannis had neither returned to the restaurant nor gone to his car. Seb wondered what was going on. If Mannis was so keen to hide the relics, could he try something provocative like confronting him up at his room? Maybe if he had someone who could confirm what was in there? A vague plan started to take shape. It was a long shot, but all that he could come up with. He borrowed a phone directory and looked up a name, then nodded as if something had reassured him that he had the right place, and checked the address against his street map.

"I'm going to find reinforcements. Call me if Mannis makes a move. I'll be back inside twenty minutes," he finished as he moved swiftly to the door. Helen, who had yet to hear who the reinforcements might be, reluctantly nodded, deciding that the well-appointed surroundings were reasonable compensation for the day's aggravation. Soon Seb was driving into the darkening evening.

He had neglected the back door. Mannis was already hurrying out of town – on foot, with a parcel under his arm. Opposite the local superstore, now closed for the night but still lit up, and by a small park, he paused to rest. He looked round. One car coming up the road, a lone jogger heading into town from the other direction. A couple of people who might remember seeing something, but wouldn't take much notice or interfere. Good. A rough voice spoke behind him. "Into the park. Now."

An extremely surprised Seb saw Mannis enter the darkened park. Having already slowed for the junction that led to the superstore, he did not accelerate as intended but stopped just up the road. Moments later he was slipping through the park gate and could hear Mannis speaking softly. Most of the oval park was lit from the store, but the top of the town-ward side, to Seb's left, was screened by shrubbery that rose above head height and the darkness was much deeper.

The voice was coming from the path by the deepest shadows. "Thanks for coming. This axe head and bracelet are sensitive, Lowry is suspicious, and I need a good excuse for losing them."

His companion laughed. "No problem. Should I just snatch them, or beat you up for added authenticity?"

Mannis proffered the parcel.

"Would you like a witness?" broke in Seb. "I don't understand what you are doing, but I will not allow you to suppress knowledge that should be public."

Mannis snarled in annoyance. "Now there's someone worth beating up." His comrade turned menacingly.

Seb needed to act fast. He dodged the unknown man and cannoned into Mannis. Both fell, and the parcel dropped to the ground with a dull clang. Mannis grabbed for it as his friend went for Seb.

Suddenly the parcel wasn't there. Seb caught a brief glimpse as another figure sprang from the shrubbery, scooped it up and made off, through the gate and up the road, too fast for middle-aged professors and relic hunters to hope to chase; especially as the latter seemed more intent on continuing the scrap, till Mannis pointed to the empty spot where the parcel had just been.

Mannis glared in disgust. He wanted to blame Lowry for allowing the theft, but in the circumstances that would hardly sound convincing. "Better let him go. This isn't the last you'll hear of the matter, Lowry." His friend threw Seb to the ground and the two stomped off.

Seb picked himself up and tidied his clothes. If anyone had remained to see him, he would have appeared surprisingly unconcerned by the turn of events. He returned to his car and his original errand. The road was empty now. Soon he was parked outside the guesthouse with the name he had noted earlier. Guessing that he had a while to wait, he phoned Helen to give her the welcome news that her vigil was over, and the less welcome news that he still had something to do before returning. A while later, the expected jogger and parcel appeared in front of his car, having taken a circuitous route back.

Seb got out. "That was some timing – especially for someone who's not on my team. What on earth were you doing there?"

Bethany was more concerned about what Seb was doing here, but: "I was just doing a run to keep fit. I saw you enter the park and thought I'd sneak in and watch. It seems you had a good reason. What were your 'friends' up to?"

Seb shook his head. "No idea. I've heard of conspiracy theories about cover-ups to stop people like you and me getting to the truth. I always thought they were nonsense. But maybe we just found one. Why hide a chapter of human history? What would there be to gain?"

Bethany ushered Seb into the lounge of the guesthouse she was using, and disappeared upstairs to change. The room was large enough for twenty or thirty people to sit comfortably, and the only other occupants were an elderly couple, who exchanged friendly greetings and then resumed their own conversation. When Bethany returned, she and Seb attacked the parcel. The contents had been cleaned; the axe head gleamed. Seb picked up the other two pieces, looked for the supposed fit, and tried it himself. Then he exclaimed in surprise.

Bethany looked, saw a reassembled bracelet but nothing significant. "What?" she prompted.

"I don't know what it means, but this is the motif I saw in Italy, the raised circle flanked by two stripes".

"Northern Italy, wasn't it?" queried Bethany.

Seb nodded. "Almost as far north as Italy gets."

Bethany seemed pleased. "Otzi the Iceman territory. That's where I've seen this sort of axe head before. It's just like the one in the Bolzano museum."

"So we've got a link between the Italian Tyrol and Cornwall," mused Seb. "And Mannis thinks that something about it is sensitive and secret. Any ideas?" He could think of none.

Bethany was equally stumped. "Cornish tin was widely traded in classical times. But two thousand years earlier...? I don't know. I suppose you'd prefer it to be nine thousand years earlier – Atlantis era?"

Seb shook his head. "One thing we do have in common – the truth is good enough for both of us."

Further discussion got them no further forward. Finally Bethany surprised Seb by offering him custody of the relics. "Maybe I might be identified," she explained, "say if Mannis comes back to the dig and sees me. But he knows you definitely don't have them, or so he thinks."

Grinning, Seb left to find his own hotel and Helen.

7

Hania

Professor Mannis sat in his well-furnished office, briefing his young assistant. "You'll remember that we've got a way of keeping tabs on Lowry. Losing that Cornwall bracelet was bad, but having it just disappear was nothing compared to the damage it could do in the wrong hands. We have good reason to believe that the logo on it was the emblem of Zeus. And Lowry has seen it on that damned carved axe in Italy."

Osgood recalled his introduction to this subject. "Zeus was the key lieutenant of the Man of Division, right?"

"Exactly. Well, *a* key lieutenant, at least. There were others." He suppressed a glower. "The rallying point against a government devoted to peace and world unity. Osiris had that in his grasp when some disaster struck him. It's taken more than four thousand years to get in sight of that goal again. What the fundamentalists would make of the Man of Division if they had his example to look back to..." He shuddered. "But back to Lowry." He produced some photographs as a memory aid. "These are the people we saw with him in Italy. Helen Carr is his girlfriend. She's purely a diversion for him, not a significant player on his team. And this is his new gap-year assistant. Josiah Hope, a Christian." He scowled. "Creationist sympathies, even. Fortunately, he can't know a great deal compared to an academic, not at this stage. He'll be very keen but won't carry much real weight.

"Now this is Josiah's brother. This is our contact point. He's a very trusting guy and we've got one of our people urging him for more information, in order to 'pray for Josiah's work'. Both Paul and our man are first-rate chess players. So they meet regularly, both online and face-to-face, and Paul tells us what Josiah's 'prayer concerns' are. He thinks he's helping his brother somehow by doing that. Of course, we know better."

"Sounds good," commented Osgood. "What 'prayer concerns' are there at the moment?"

"Lowry has got it clear in his head that there's something important on Malta. He's making preparations for a substantial search. But the Hope boys know nothing specific. Quite possibly it's still a needle in a haystack business. I get the impression that Lowry has some significant clue but can't actually construe it. If so, we just watch – no need to intervene and risk drawing attention to ourselves, unless Lowry gets a break. As he nearly did, in Cornwall." Another scowl. "But he has a more immediate agenda on Crete. He's taking Josiah there next week. Some contact in the former capital, Hania, has tipped him off about something. We have no details of the find, except that the news came in response to a Lowry e-mail, asking if anyone recognised a circle and stripes logo. It seems that Lowry somehow got a description of the bracelet that I saw in Cornwall, and tied it in with the Italian axe. So we don't want to take a chance on this one.

"We do know that Josiah has a plane ticket to Heraklion on the afternoon of Wednesday next week, and a room booked nearby overnight. They'll be in Hania on Thursday, but not until the afternoon. Lowry has promised to show him round the ruins of Knossos first. You get there first – there's direct travel arranged already – pass yourself off as Hope, and say that Lowry's indisposed and can you borrow the find to show him. It's lucky that you look young enough to pass as a student. Here's a plan of the town, and this is the dig site. Then the find just disappears, and no one will know what's happened to it. You don't have to travel back with it – just give it to a contact who will also provide you with a car over there – nowhere near the dig. Dead simple – the only thing you have to do is call yourself Josiah Hope."

"Sure," agreed Osgood confidently. "I can't see any problem with that. By the way, do we know what the emblem actually is, and what it's doing in Western Europe?"

Mannis thought. "I don't know what to make of it so far west. Trading links, perhaps. There are traditions – you'll be initiated into them someday. I thought that the opposition to Osiris was centred on the eastern Mediterranean. But one of the figures in it is described as being from the northern mountains. Maybe that meant the Alps, though they ought to be western rather than northern, from Osiris' perspective. North-west, possibly. And I think Lowry isn't too far wrong with his idea about it being a sun sign."

One evening in early October, Josiah sought out Bethany after the church service. After a brief exchange of pleasantries, he came straight to the point. "Would you fancy a couple of days of Mediterranean sun?"

Bethany had no idea what to make of this. "Er... is this business or pleasure?" she asked at length. She wasn't sure she wanted either alternative.

Josiah reddened, realising that he'd not made his meaning plain. "Strictly business. Seb Lowry and I were off to Crete to check out a new discovery. Something pre-Minoan, from an area known as Kydonia, he tells me. But he's double-booked himself and can't go. He wants me to fly out anyway and take a look. But I'm new to this stuff; I mean, I've read a bit, but I wouldn't really know what I was looking at. I'm hoping you could give me a hand, maybe save me from looking a fool."

Bethany smelt a rat. Was Seb manipulating this situation in a ploy to get her on side? Although she had resolved to try to be open to God's leading, this did not feel right. "I am not working for Lowry," she said emphatically, trying hard not to sound too snappy.

Josiah just grinned. "That's OK, he won't need to pay you then. I imagine he'd cover your expenses though."

Bethany's instinct said a very definite no, but to avoid offence she said that she would think it over. She didn't really mean it. All the arguments against working with Lowry were as strong in her mind as ever. Surely God would not put her through three years of hard study only to throw the fruits away. She mentioned it in her prayer time, just in a token way. There was no direct answer. But slowly, over the next twenty-four hours, another thought grew in her mind. Maybe it *was* from the Lord, though at the time she didn't realise it. Could she refuse to help out a fellow believer, when she had nothing better to do? Could she be sure this was not God's doing? Her professional curiosity also asserted itself. Reluctantly, half feeling she was making a mistake, she phoned Josiah and agreed to go with him.

The flight out to Crete was uneventful. Something delayed the unloading of luggage, not that they had much with them. They seemed to concentrate on the baggage carousel for so long that it began to seem that the belt was still and the floor on which they stood was moving past it. Fortunately they were not short of time. By evening they were settled in cheap lodgings near the centre of town.

The next morning they caught an early bus west from Heraclion. Knossos was off the agenda; Bethany had been there and dismissively described it as unscientific speculative reconstruction work. The day was fine and clear, the sunlight bright enough to dazzle unaccustomed eyes. They were grateful for the few high clouds, which promised to take the edge off the heat. To their right they had frequent views of the sea. Southward the land rose in many steep hills, and behind them the great bulk of Mount Psiloritis was visible. Despite the autumn heat at sea level, in a few weeks the upper reaches of the 8000ft mountain would be shrouded in snow. Josiah checked their progress on a map as they passed the coastal resorts, pointing out places he'd seen there.

Josiah was curious about how Bethany had come to Seb's attention. To pass the time, she told him the story. A fellow student had mentioned that Seb was pushing the line that the Sphinx went back to a lost civilization around 10000 BC. "CHEOPS refuted that several years ago. Our latest work indicates that the Sphinx is slightly older than the pyramids, but the supposed Ice Age water erosion is just natural drainage from the third millennium BC, the way the site was before the pyramids went up. I mugged up on the research and confronted Seb with questions from the floor, after his presentation. To give him credit, once he was satisfied I knew what I was talking about, he wanted to know more. He took down all my references. I think there will be a correction in his next book."

"Cheops? I thought he was a Pharaoh, not a researcher," queried Josiah.

"Comparative History of Egypt and Other Pyramid-building Societies," explained Bethany. "A rather contrived acronym, but it's a research group. I've been a member since I started university. I've done brief trips to Egypt and Mexico with them – subsidised, fortunately."

Shortly before midday, they disembarked at Hania bus station. Working from a combination of map and memory, Josiah guided them through the former island capital, down towards the harbour. There he looked for the street to the nearby excavation site. When he'd last seen the place, only Minoan remains had been unearthed, but in recent times some deeper trenches had been dug. Slowly he deciphered the Greek letters on the street sign, confirming their route. "This way," he directed. "Just up this road, on the left." Bethany demurred, wanting a short delay; she was busy taking tourist snaps. Josiah, eager to complete Seb's mission, strode off anyway. "See you in a minute. You can't get lost from here."

As Josiah approached the site, another man emerged from the side-gate, carrying a package. A member of the site team called after him, "Goodbye, Mr Hope." Mr Hope? This was an odd coincidence. He looked closely at the man, realizing he'd seen him before, trying to place where.

Vic Osgood noticed the teenager checking him over. Having seen a photo as a reminder, he recognised him at once – Seb Lowry's young assistant, the guy he was impersonating. He couldn't risk discovery now that he had the goods. He dodged past Josiah and starting running towards the harbour.

Josiah realized that something was up. He turned and gave chase, yelling for Bethany to help. Her name meant nothing to Osgood, till he saw her moving to intercept him. Evading traffic, he dodged left into a side street. He was looking for a right turn back to the harbour, but a couple of motorcyclists in his path forced him the other way. Looking back, he saw Bethany gaining on him, the young sportswoman settling into a practised stride. Josiah was into the chase too. He needed a diversion.

Osgood bounded up steps into the crowded market building, scattering a couple of beggars at the north entrance. He was still heading inland, the wrong way for his purpose. He barged through a crowd of locals and tourists, then saw the chance to make the right turn that he wanted, through the fish section of the market. Grabbing a loose tray of fish and aiming it somewhere near Bethany's feet, he dashed for the western exit.

Josiah had vaguely remembered the cross-shaped layout of the market. Guessing that Osgood was still hoping to double back towards the harbour, he had not tracked him but moved to cut him off. At the western exit he loomed suddenly in front of Osgood, arms spread wide to block the path. Osgood charged straight into him, knocking him over, escaping down to the street. Now he could follow the zigzagging roads back to the harbour. Josiah picked himself up and gave chase once more.

Bethany stumbled over the fish tray, and felt obliged to pause to offer apologies. As soon as she could, she rejoined the pursuit, seeing Josiah and gaining on him, hoping that he still had their opponent in sight.

Osgood lengthened his stride as the slope towards the harbour started to favour him, slight though it was. He was drenched in sweat, beginning to struggle for breath, but determination and a fear of letting his mentor down kept him going. At the harbour the sea breeze was strong enough to be refreshing. He swung left past a string of seafront restaurants, too spent to appreciate the Venetian heritage all around him as he sped past.

Now Josiah remembered the car park from his previous visit, just out of sight beyond the further exit of the harbour frontage.

That must be the goal. Suddenly, with a ringing of bells, a horse and carriage passed straight in front of him, tourists on board. Shocked, he checked his stride, then darted round the carriage and onward, Bethany now almost on his heels. Osgood glanced round and saw he had gained more of a lead.

Bethany figured her fitness would let her catch the man who was fleeing from them, if there was no more interference. She was less sure what she could do next, not knowing who the guy was. She needed Josiah to help with that part. She swept past him and then slowed enough to keep just a pace ahead. "Track me," she called over her shoulder.

Josiah, beginning to labour, realised he now had the advantage of a pacesetter to follow. "Got to catch him at the corner," he panted. He saw Bethany nod. She was reeling Osgood in with each stride, but at a rate that Josiah could stay with.

The trio chased around the quayside, still dodging past many people on the path between cafés and water. Beyond the last restaurant the path became suddenly clear. Osgood tried to put on speed to complete his escape, but the lack of obstacles was in his pursuers' favour. Bethany had the training, the stamina, and ultimately the pace. As they rounded the entrance to the harbour, turning left, a car appeared suddenly in front of them. Osgood instinctively sidestepped right, towards the water's edge. Bethany, with a second longer to react, veered left, taking the inside line. She was ahead of him at last.

Osgood looked round, and saw Josiah closing fast. He tried to turn and dodge, but there was no room to manoeuvre. He tumbled over a bollard and crashed into the water. The package spun out of his grasp.

Josiah leapt down on to rocks that broke the surface, stooped, and snatched the package from the shallows as Osgood floundered. He climbed up again, no longer interested in Osgood, and showed it to Bethany. Immediately the package had all their attention.

Osgood hauled himself out of the water and slipped away, cursing his misfortune, but grateful that no one wanted to stop him and challenge his false identity. He could hardly go on claiming to be Josiah Hope with the real one present.

A few passers-by had seen the end of the chase and were looking on with curiosity. Bethany sensed that an explanation was called for. "That man was a thief," she offered between deep breaths.

Josiah took up the tale. "Valuable pre-Minoan artefact," indicating the package. He gasped. "We are to take it to Heraclion – to the archaeological museum." It was enough to satisfy the onlookers.

They reviewed the position over lunch, sitting inconspicuously by a wall inside one of the harbour restaurants. Should they just return the package to the site it had come from? "Osgood was pretending to be me. So the site crew have given 'me' permission to have it. But taking it off-site wasn't part of the original deal. I wonder what excuse he gave?… If we go back there, will they believe we're Seb's real representatives, if they think that Osgood's me?"

Bethany hated the thought of becoming some sort of relic hunter, on the borderline of legality. But remembering her experience in Cornwall, she wasn't sure whom they could safely trust. They had to get the package examined before returning it. In the end they decided that Josiah's inspiration on the harbour front was a good idea. Making sure that Osgood was nowhere to be seen, they caught the bus back to Heraclion.

Somewhere along the coastal highway, a furiously driven hire car went speeding past the bus. The motorist, now back in dry clothes, failed to spot Josiah and Bethany as he passed.

Back in their rooms in Heraclion, they eagerly yielded to mounting excitement and opened the package. Bethany insisted this was done carefully, well aware of the risk of damaging the contents. Inside were some shards of pottery, wrapped with paper and padding that seemed to have been thrown together hastily; it was apparent that the package had only been made up because Osgood had insisted on removing the material. The shards were broken; but it was easy to see how they fitted together to make a larger fragment. Flecks of dull paint still clung to the clay. A pattern showed around what would have once been part of the rim. It was the pattern from the Cornwall bracelet, the motif Seb and Josiah had seen in the Tyrol, now revealed in patches of colour still visible after so many millennia. The circle was white, the background deepest blue, and at either side was a vertical yellow stripe. But it was the figure below, seen only as an etched outline, which grabbed their attention; a pile of stones – perhaps an altar – with an animal on it, and a man with arm raised to strike. Above the sacrifice was an arch of many lines. The same thought struck both of them.

"A rainbow – Noah's sacrifice and the rainbow covenant after the flood!" exclaimed Josiah.

"Could be," agreed Bethany, wondering about the implications. "A biblical motif, pre-Minoan from what Seb was told, so well over three thousand years old. It could even be older than the Exodus – ancient and independent support for the Bible story. That's significant in itself, though I'm not sure it will do much for Seb."

"What's it doing in Crete?"

"Trade, maybe. There was trade between Egypt and Crete. The Israelites were in Egypt; maybe it's Israelite make, say about the time of Joseph. But that's just a guess at this stage," concluded Bethany cautiously.

"Someone who owned a pot like this may well have been a believer," mused Josiah.

Bethany wasn't going to jump to a conclusion. "Perhaps. The potter, or whoever commissioned the decoration, must have at least known the story. The Cretan owner might just have liked the shape of the pot."

Josiah was keen to speculate. "Well, I think they were the good guys."

Bethany raised an eyebrow. "Who?"

"Whoever owned a picture of the rainbow covenant. And whoever used this white circle motif we keep finding."

Bethany just grinned. "If you can sustain that level of imagination, I'm sure you'll get on Seb's staff permanently."

The next morning, Josiah appeared at breakfast with an air of gloom hanging over him. He had phoned Seb in England and the news was lousy. Mannis (Seb presumed) had pulled strings, and there was a serious fuss. "Two British tourists have stolen a precious artefact. Osgood has been airbrushed out of the picture. Seb expects us to be arrested at the airport."

Bethany tried to lighten the atmosphere. "Heraclion or Gatwick?" Josiah just groaned. "Both, probably."

"We only took the thing to keep it out of Mannis's clutches," mused Bethany, hoping to find inspiration as to a way out. "Our brief was only to look at it. I suppose we have stolen it, but with mitigating circumstances. Why don't we just return it? After all, you did say that we were taking it to the Heraclion museum."

"But don't we want it for Seb's research?" objected Josiah.

Bethany saw no problem. "Ideally, yes. But we've examined it, we know what it looks like, we've got photographs."

Josiah looked at her in surprise. "Photographs?"

Bethany grinned faintly. "Of course. I took them in my room this morning. It's the sort of thing professionals do; I wouldn't expect Seb to have thought of suggesting it."

They phoned Seb again and agreed a strategy. Later that morning a correction buzzed along the news wires. British author Seb Lowry denied that his assistant had stolen anything; in fact the said assistant had thwarted an attempt by an impersonator to purloin the object in question. The said object was temporarily in safekeeping and would be returned shortly. There was no word on the identity of the actual would-be thief. Seb was saving that knowledge for another occasion.

Having allowed enough time for this to disseminate, Josiah and Bethany approached the museum. Coming from the south, across the wide space of the Plateia Eleftherias, they had a good view before they could be recognised. They were relieved to see no sign of Osgood, but as they drew near they spotted a small group of media reporters. Bethany hesitated. "I'm here as your friend. I'm not putting myself up as Lowry's representative."

Josiah was not fazed. "That's OK. I can handle the talking. You stay on the side and watch."

Bethany was both delighted and surprised by this. "Thanks, I appreciate that. You are sure it will be all right?"

"I used to be secretary to the local youth wing of UKIP. I've spoken in public, and to the press occasionally." With stride reflecting his confident words, Josiah took the re-wrapped package and walked forward. Bethany loitered nearby as Josiah announced himself.

Immediately the press were around Josiah, firing questions. He answered smoothly. "No, I'm not a thief. I retrieved the pottery and have brought it here for safekeeping... I only came here to view it, which I've done... No question of keeping it myself... Would you like to see it?"

Suddenly a museum staff member intervened firmly. "Mr Hope, just hand the package over. It's for the museum to display it in due course." Josiah had to hand it over, still sealed. The staff member retreated into the museum. A couple of photographers frowned at the missed opportunity.

The press seemed about to disperse, but then one of the reporters tried a last query, a final attempt to entice a story out of what now seemed a trivial incident. "Have you anything else to say?"

Josiah's political instincts came to the fore. "Well, like many other British people, I'm proud of my own country's heritage. So I fully respect your similar pride in your own culture and heritage, and your desire to keep control of its symbols. I hope that the independent peoples of Britain and Greece will always be friends."

The reporters liked what they were hearing. One of them pressed for more. "Does that mean you think that Britain should return the Elgin Marbles?"

Bethany was close enough to hear the question and see that Josiah was flummoxed. He was frantically searching his memory, finding no clue as to what the Elgin Marbles might be. There was no choice now. Muttering resignedly, she stepped to his side and whispered a quick briefing. "They're relics from the Parthenon, now in the British Museum. The Greeks want them back." Josiah asked a quick question, and she answered it.

Josiah faced the reporter again. "Well, er, of course it's not my decision. But if it were – I guess, on that principle, yes – I would return them."

The press had what they wanted.

8

Aftermath

The plane climbing out of Heraclion airport banked sharply right. For a moment Bethany suspected an emergency, but the angle of ascent stayed constant and she realised the turn was intentional. The plane was now heading out over the sea instead of along the built-up coast. Inwardly she was still fuming that she'd had to intervene in the press call. She wanted to be taken seriously in her chosen career. She wished she'd never heard of Lowry. She didn't want her life veering in unexpected directions.

Suddenly, without any inward volition, a picture flashed into her mind: the mighty power of God propelling her onwards like the engines of the plane, wings of angels bearing her on high. She realised God wouldn't be fazed by a change of course. In that instant spirit and mind agreed on a decision. It wasn't an expected one, but somehow it now suddenly seemed right, seemed to be what had been planned all along. The doubts still remained below the surface, but the anxiety flowing from them was answered. She shook her head in wonderment at how easily God could rearrange the jumble of her life.

At Gatwick both the travellers were in high spirits. Mission accomplished, opposition foiled, another clue to study. They collected their bags and headed for the exit. There was little formality for passengers arriving from within the European Union.

"Hold it!" There was no arguing with the clear and determined order. They found themselves surrounded by security staff, ushered into the new antiterrorist facility, and checked for weapons. Bethany's camera was found and confiscated, requests for an explanation ignored. Something was said about Schedule 7, which meant nothing to either of them. Soon they were away from the crowds, isolated, alarmed. The facility looked clinical, efficient, with guards posted at regular intervals. It was clearly meant to intimidate any suspect. Totally at a loss, they were shut in an interview room, left to brew over the situation; for how long they could not know. Both guessed that the room was bugged, in case they might incriminate themselves in discussing an alibi. Glad they had nothing criminal to hide, they speculated briefly nevertheless. They could guess that Osgood might be responsible, but what reason could he have given? Unable to fathom the situation, Bethany fell silent. Josiah hummed a worship song to keep his spirits up.

A burly officer of West Indian descent entered the room. Bethany looked up; Josiah just kept on humming, trying to portray an air of relaxed innocence. The man came and stood over them, authoritative, threatening. Suddenly he hesitated as if something didn't quite fit. His first question was unexpected: "What are you humming?"

Josiah had no idea why it should matter, but he named the tune.

"Do you know the words?" came the next question.

"Of course." Josiah quoted the chorus, baffled as to where this was leading.

"How about..." He named another popular Christian worship song.

Josiah wasn't quite sure; he looked at Bethany.

She knew it well. "I've sung it more often at Reading than at home. But you must remember it too." She started singing softly. Josiah's memory clicked and he joined in.

The security officer eyed them warily. "Those are Christian songs," he commented. Josiah nodded.

Bethany stopped short. Trying to suppress the sarcasm that she was aware came too frequently to her voice, to be suitably respectful and conciliatory, she asked, "Is this an interrogation or a worship session?"

"I'm asking the questions, Miss Fisher. Tell me one of your favourite Bible passages." Bethany, puzzled, obliged with a verse that she used when witnessing, and a short testimony to illustrate it. The officer stared at her. "We got a tip-off that you were Al Qaeda sympathisers, converts to Islam carrying photos that could compromise British security. But you are clearly practising Christians."

Now they were all surprised. "Would you like to check with our pastor?" offered Josiah.

The officer considered. "He could identify you?"

Josiah and Bethany both nodded.

"Sounds like a good way to verify your identities." He produced Bethany's camera from a pocket. "I suppose I'd still better ask: what's on the camera?"

Bethany hesitated momentarily, but could see no reason to dissemble. "Just archaeological material and tourist snaps. I'm an archaeology graduate. Josiah works for Seb Lowry – the author of Ancient Quest, you know. I was with him in Crete on a sort of freelance basis, before taking up a more permanent post that Mr Lowry's offered me. Er, would you like Mr Lowry to identify us too?"

The officer laughed. "I think that would be superfluous. This is clearly a case of mistaken identity. But we will need to confirm it before we let you go. Still, I guess there's no point in handing the camera to our technical team now." He took their pastor's address, returned the camera, and left them alone again.

They were still bemused, but Josiah had a different question. "Why did you say that you will be working for Seb Lowry?"

"I made up my mind on the flight back," answered Bethany. "Whatever it is we've got ourselves into, I'm now identified as being on Lowry's side in it. So I might as well take his money. If it wrecks my career, well, I guess God's set up the situation, and he'll have to sort it out."

Josiah turned mock formal. "I'm very pleased to meet you, my new colleague," he grinned.

A couple of hours later, having completed the formalities, they were being driven home by their pastor. He was very intrigued by the whole story. "I want to see this rainbow covenant scene," he insisted.

"Fine," said Bethany, "but we may want to keep it out of the religious press for the moment, please. Lowry's income depends on his books. He'll want to choose his moment for the publicity."

In another part of London, Vic Osgood was being taken to task. "You tried to frame two Christians as Islamic terrorists?" demanded Mannis.

"It was all I could think of at short notice," blustered Osgood. "It didn't need to stand up in court, just get any pictures out of their hands temporarily and 'accidentally' delete them, to make sure they had no proof of what they saw. Our man in the security team must have the pics by now."

"No," said the humanist group official whom Osgood had met previously. "The man who interrogated them was another Christian. He saw through your allegation before he got as far as passing the camera on for analysis. It happens like that sometimes. These *Christians*" – he made it sound like a swear word – "seem to have some sixth sense for identifying one another; maybe a common air they all catch from their religious rituals. Anyway, he realised it was a false alarm, and just gave the camera back untouched."

Osgood swore, several times. He hated to admit it but, "I guess I screwed up. How much harm has it done? Do we have a comeback?"

Mannis was reassuring. "You were unlucky. Another minute or so in Hania and Josiah Hope would have missed you. And there aren't many Christians in airport security. Still, it may not be as bad as it looks."

Osgood wanted to agree, but had his doubts. "But the fragments they showed me in Hania – the picture of Noah's sacrifice – won't the Christians make a big play with that? We can't easily explain it away." He noticed that Mannis was still smiling. "Can we?"

"Oh yes, with any luck. It will go down a storm in Christian circles, but they all believe, whether they think they have evidence or not. The big snag is that it might make them wonder what else could be out there if they look for it, which could be a longer term problem. That was the worry which led us to send you on this mission. We will have to be more careful that nothing shows up to corroborate this. But on its own, it probably won't have much impact outside the churches." Osgood was still looking extremely sceptical. "It's like that cylinder seal in the British Museum, showing Adam and Eve being tempted by the serpent to eat from the forbidden tree. We can't get it packed away because some academics would wonder why, but we've got it labelled as a banqueting scene. Hardly any visitors realise what it's really showing. Surprising how deep into Mesopotamian culture some of the Hebrew myths go, if you think about it."

"Which people don't," added the humanist. "Think about it, that is."

Osgood gaped. "You're kidding," he asserted. Mannis and the humanist shook their heads. "There's evidence for the Garden of Eden on show in the British Museum?" he demanded. "And you allow it?"

"Calm down. Yes, it's in the Mesopotamian galleries. Don't worry, it's been sitting there for years; it's proven completely harmless. At worst it's just an indication that a myth is a bit older than we'd like it to be."

Seb celebrated the completion of his team by treating them to a trip to the Historic Dockyard at Portsmouth. Josiah took in tours of HMS Victory and Warrior, while Bethany enjoyed a study of the latest restoration work on the Mary Rose. Although her main interests lay well before the sixteenth century, the state-of-the-art preservation techniques were fascinating. She wondered how well they might work on more ancient underwater remains.

When Seb and Helen returned from a boat trip round the harbour, the quartet reunited for lunch. Josiah was still enthralled by the Victory exhibition. "I never knew that Nelson had a Christian background," he commented. "He seems to have treated his officers and men better than many other commanders did; it was one of the reasons for his popularity."

Bethany raised her eyebrows. "I thought he ran off with another man's wife."

"So he did. But we both know that one flaw doesn't disqualify someone from being a Christian. He fell short in one way, but his faith shone through in others."

Seb was still uncomfortable with the religious interests of his team members. He changed the subject to one of his own choosing. "What would you say is the most sensational thing on display here?" He listened patiently while Bethany explained the preservation work, and Josiah expressed his pride in the great naval heritage of Britain. But at length he shook his head, and produced two rolled up plastic sheets from his bag. He unwrapped one. It was rather less than two feet by one and a half, an illustrated map of Europe. "Try this. Actually it's not on display nowadays, but it's the sort of map used on the Mary Rose, and it used to be sold at the gift shop. But the illustrations were done with south at the top, so they displayed it upside down. Unless you knew what you're looking for, you missed the point. The giveaway is these compass designs – they're known as wind roses – with the grid lines radiating from them to show the bearings. This is what's known as a portolan map. You recognise this bit?" He turned the map so that south faced towards Bethany and Josiah.

"The Med, obviously," said Josiah.

"Of course. And here?" Seb pointed to the left side of the map, just above halfway up.

Josiah's eyes widened. "It has to be Britain. The south coast is clear, you can even see the Isle of Wight – but the rest – it's not much more accurate than a squiggle."

"And Scandinavia looks completely wrong," put in Bethany. Her eyes wandered back to Britain. "Just a minute. The Channel looks fine, Brittany, the Lizard, and so on. But what's this vast river in Normandy? The Seine was never that large."

"Try the Rhine, over in Germany," replied Seb easily, pointing to another river, then more rivers in turn. "Or the Nile. Or this one here" – pointing to the Black Sea – "I think it's called the Dneiper."

Josiah was recalling the relevant part of Ancient Quest. "This is what you argue was mapped long, long ago – before the estuaries that we know today had been deposited? I read it and was intrigued – but to actually see it like this is amazing." He shook his head, wondering.

Seb turned to Bethany, his demeanour seeming to challenge her to raise an objection. Well, that was her function in the team.

Suddenly she grinned. "There is one rather large problem though." Seb waited. "The gift shop now stocks globes printed with maps in this sort of style. There were even some of those wind roses on them. But I thought you might be interested, so I asked if they were based on genuine Mary Rose-era globes. They weren't. Just an artist's impression. Maybe your map here is the same."

Seb was deflated. He thought rapidly. "Well maybe... I thought I checked for the source..." He scanned the map again. Some small print in the margin by the NW corner caught his eye. He rotated the map and picked it up to read it better. "Aha! It's a 1992 copy, but the original dates from 1542 and is held by the British Library. So, not just an artist's impression. It's been done in an artistic style, but the map is genuine."

He waited for Bethany to try again, confident that it was a tough challenge. She stalled for time: "It does look convincing." Then something occurred to her. "But the coasts are drawn a lot more jaggedly than on a modern map. I could argue that the large estuaries are just exaggerated jaggedness."

Seb looked at her, but said nothing. She looked back. Did she really believe that her argument was valid? Was there anything to bolster it? "Drawn in 1542 then. Four hundred and seventy three years ago. And the point you're dying to make would be that surveying then was lousy. No way to find longitude is the punch line, isn't it? See, I have been swotting up on your work."

"No. I still don't see that you have a total picture – and you need one. But on the face of it, you win this round."

She rolled the map up and handed it to Seb. He declined it. "I've already got one at home, along with a couple of other similar ones. These are for you two."

From time to time, Seb sent out a newsletter to update those of his readers who had asked to be informed of developments in his investigations. Josiah was in the project office, editing the latest edition, when Seb appeared in a very excited mood. "I've been poring through the ancient stories," he exclaimed, "looking for any reference that might relate to the Treasures of Zeus."

Bethany, visiting for a final planning session for the Malta excursion, looked up from reading an academic magazine she'd brought with her. She wasn't impressed by Seb's enthusiasm for digging out occasional nuggets from mythology. "Do we climb Mount Olympus and start digging into the summit?"

Seb sighed. "No. But Zeus and his cronies, whoever they might have been originally, are said to have fought a war with a group called Titans. And at least one ancient source says that the Titans were based at Mount Etna in Sicily and were led by Atlas."

Bethany shrugged, not interested in fables.

Josiah tried to connect Seb's statement to other things in their research, but failed. "So?"

"Well, Atlas was the ruler of Atlantis. And look at the map. Supposing there was an Atlantic-based power expanding in the western Mediterranean, and it had got to the point of striking for Greece as in Plato's account, where would it launch the attack from?"

Josiah got up and studied the chart on the wall briefly. "I see what you're getting at. In Atlas's place, you'd want a forward base, and if your next target is Greece, then your current frontline is Italy or Sicily."

Seb nodded. "It's the same story that Plato was telling, just one is in mythical terms and the other is presented as history. The general outline is the same – an attack on Greece from the west. There has to be something real underlying it."

"And in this scenario," put in Bethany drily, "who has control of Malta?"

"Atlas, obviously," said Josiah as he glanced at the map again. "Malta is directly below Si... Oh! You're wondering how these Treasures of Zeus can wind up somewhere that Zeus's lot don't have access to."

"Fired across the sea by lightning bolt, perhaps," smirked Bethany. "Zeus's lightning bolt crops up in a lot of myths, you know. There has to be something real underlying it. Or is your methodology flawed?"

Seb was thinking hard. Had he gone down a dead end? He looked to the rhyme translation from the Piali map, also pinned to the office wall. "One moment. The treasures were hidden after Zeus's children defeated Atlas. They were hidden from Osiris. The western enemy was gone, and now the west was safe and the danger was from the east; Malta had become a safe refuge. Yes. Zeus's side had gained access to Malta because Atlantis was destroyed."

Bethany in turn considered this. "I suppose it's a possibility," she conceded reluctantly. "But you're talking about a massive geopolitical event, war between Atlantis and whoever was then in power in Greece – and a massive geological event, the physical destruction of an island empire – and you need both to happen at pretty much the same time. It's just too much of a coincidence."

"Probably true," admitted Seb, "though if it did happen like that, it would explain why Zeus, Athena and the other fighters were made into gods. As the story was told and retold, the humans who just happened to be in the right place to benefit from the disaster morphed into divine beings with the power to wield the forces of nature. Naturally falling rocks became hundred-handed monsters throwing them at will."

"Athena a fighter?" queried Josiah.

"Yes," said Seb, "the myths put her right in the frontline, though fighting more by wit than by brute strength. It's another recurring theme in the ancient stories: Amazons at the Trojan War, Camilla in Virgil."

"If you just wait a moment," added Bethany, "he'll tell you that there has to be something real underlying it."

"Exactly!"

"No way," said Bethany emphatically. "Imagine me going up against Kompany and Toure. However much I work on my skills, there are physical limitations which mean it wouldn't work. It's not as if Athena could have had a tank or a battery of missiles to fight with. There could be no woman on the frontline of a prehistoric battle."

Josiah had a one word counter. "Neanderthal."

"What?"

Josiah explained. "I read once about a female Neanderthal fossil which had its muscle attachments analysed. The conclusion was that she would have been stronger than the typical modern man. So if Athena was a Neanderthal..."

"...she'd have been dead about thirty thousand years before all this supposedly happened," finished Bethany.

Josiah thought about a riposte, but decided it wouldn't be helpful. He slumped back looking deflated.

9

Clues

Josiah, Paul and Bethany stepped on to the sole platform of a little-used Cornish station. They were the only passengers to alight. They filed out through the ticket office and immediately spotted the man they had come to see, standing at ease beside a small, dark car. He was wearing a habit like a monk, though the Christian community he belonged to was not a strict monastic order. On catching sight of the trio, he glanced for reference at a small photograph, then nodded a greeting.

"I'm B-brother Simon," he stammered.

"Paul Hope," acknowledged Paul.

It was noticeable that neither extended a hand to the other. Paul introduced his brother and Bethany.

"How long have we been corresponding?" asked the man. "I've been looking forward to seeing you for a long time."

"It's been three years, four months and twenty one days," replied Paul. Josiah winced at the unnecessary level of detail, so typical of his brother's condition. "I would have liked to have come before, but the journey across London is difficult for me. Too many people and too much noise. I needed a reason to bring my friends with me for support."

Simon nodded again. "I understand, of course. Noise is a problem for me too – I've told you that in my letters. At the community there is quiet, and freedom from the stress of daily living.

Also, they accept that I don't have a girlfriend. You will like it there."

Was it just imagination that at the word 'girlfriend', Paul's eyes seemed to flash momentarily in Bethany's direction. "I'm getting paranoid," she told herself.

They piled into the car, overnight bags in the boot, and set off down some narrow, twisting country lanes. After about fifteen minutes they turned on to a secluded drive, leading to the community site, a set of low brick buildings surrounding a central stone chapel. Simon led them into a kitchen and made some coffee. He introduced another community member who was cleaning up. Others of his group were busy around the site, tending to a small number of animals and a vegetable garden.

"We try to be as self-sufficient as possible," explained Simon. "It makes for healthier eating too. In fact one of our newer members had been plagued with stomach trouble for some months before joining us. He'd been treated for IBS, but it hadn't helped. As soon as he came here, his symptoms cleared up."

"Something in the diet?" queried Paul.

"Well, he put it down to God's blessing. Then one day a visitor gave us a little packet of snack-sized omelettes. Joe ate a couple and his stomach trouble returned."

"What on earth can be in an omelette to cause that?" exclaimed Bethany, as memories of a food poisoning incident at University came flooding back.

"That was our reaction too. We checked the ingredient list – there wasn't much to it – and the only thing that stood out was something called rapeseed oil. We don't have Internet here, but one of our friends ran an online search for us, and sure enough, some people have reported an intolerance to rapeseed oil. And apparently it's getting used in more and more products nowadays, so people like Joe who have coped with it all their lives are suddenly finding it's a problem."

After coffee they proceeded to the place where a new set of guest quarters was being prepared. The community didn't like to charge for providing a spiritual service as a retreat and prayer centre, but they did have to accept some money to cover costs. Simon explained that this was where, while digging the foundations, they had found a large stone tablet with writing in Latin. Bethany wanted to see the exact spot, but it was now covered by the foundation work. Determined to get some documentation, she settled for drawing a quick sketch of the main features in the landscape.

Then Simon led them to the chapel. The tablet was stored in a side room; Simon brought it out and laid it on a table for inspection. On the left was a drawing of an oak tree, beside it fragments of writing in etched capitals. The right side was jagged.

"Broken," observed Josiah.

"This sort of find usually is," responded Bethany, unconcerned.

"We believe the tree is a symbol of Druids, and this is their writing," explained Simon.

Josiah pulled out his phone and got Seb on the line. He described what they were looking at.

Seb picked up on the Druid reference. "That doesn't fit – the Druid tradition was purely oral – not written down."

Paul was staring at the middle of the tree, where four branches emerged in an X shape from the same point. Above it there was a sort of loop in the right hand side of the trunk. "See that? I think it's a Chi Rho symbol worked into the drawing. It's not Druid at all."

Seb's voice came over the phone, demanding to know what a Chi Rho symbol was. Paul explained that it was an early Christian way of representing the first two Greek letters of the title "Christ".

Seb pondered, speculating. "But there is a tree too. So maybe it's a Christian and a Druid symbol at the same time? Perhaps a Christian writer, who was sympathetic to the Druid tradition but not bound by their insistence on not writing it down? What does Bethany say?"

Josiah passed the phone over. Bethany thought, and replied slowly, "There was a Roman writer – Pliny, I think – who said something about Druids having to do with oaks. Wood nymphs were called Dryads, and Y in Latin corresponds to U in Greek, so 'Druad' would be related to trees. I don't know if anything confirms Pliny's information."

"OK," said Seb's voice. "So suppose it's some sort of hybrid symbol, from both Druid and Christian traditions. What about the writing with it? Can you tell if it's genuine?"

"My Latin is a bit rusty," admitted Bethany, sifting through her bag for a Latin dictionary, which she then referred to as she read the stone. "*MDC*, what kind of word is that? Oh, it's a number, of course. Sixteen hundred… er, *years before Brutus.* Then the line is broken. Next line: *Iulanus his forefather, son of Zeus…* What is this? Any fool knows that Zeus is a Greek name. The Romans called him Jupiter. It's a fake, Seb."

"But we are interested in Zeus," pointed out Seb over the phone. "What if Zeus is the right name and Jupiter is some sort of translation? That could make this fragment important."

Bethany sighed heavily and took another look at it. "*Iulanus son of Zeus… the strong, to Lyonesse came.* Then a break again. Next line: *Shushanna* – good Roman name that, Shushan was in Persia … *Shushanna of the north mountains, they attacked ships of the kings of the sea…* gap… *eagle* – or battle standard – *moon bright as the sky darkens*, then an incomplete phrase… Last line: *by a stratagem Lyonesse they saved.* Make what you will of that."

"The kings of the sea?" queried Josiah. The phrase had sparked his interest, as well as Seb's.

"And a son of Zeus," added Seb's voice. "This could be the same story we've been looking at, of the children of Zeus vanquishing Atlas and his Titans. Iulanus the strong or mighty man… I wonder what his name is in the mythology. Maybe Apollo, or Ares…"

"If you're going down that route," broke in Bethany, "keep in mind that the word for 'strong' is in the plural. It's talking about more than one strong man."

"Neanderthals," muttered Josiah. He saw Bethany roll her eyes and didn't pursue the thought.

At that point Simon broke into the conversation. "I'm sorry but we have to leave the chapel now; there is a gathering for prayer starting."

Paul immediately asked why they couldn't join in the prayers. Simon looked surprised for a moment but then nodded. He had been so focussed on the discussion about the stone inscription that he had overlooked that the visitors might have other interests too.

"Seb, we have to go now. Call you later," said Bethany.

"OK," came the response, "but I want you and Josiah to see if you can find out anything more on these characters Brutus, Iulanus and Shushanna, once you're back in London."

Bethany's glare was obvious even down the phone. "Brutus was the guy who killed Julius Caesar. I think he was defeated by Augustus after that. Iulanus and Shushanna never existed. Well, I grant you that Iulanus could be some minor Roman. But anyone called Shushanna belongs in the Middle East, not Rome, and nowhere near Britain."

The trio stayed overnight with the community, then made the return train journey the next afternoon. It was with considerable reluctance that Bethany showed up at Josiah's home on the morning after that. She found him already logged on to the Net, and surrounded by books and papers. "You surely aren't taking this seriously?" she asked with typical sarcasm.

Josiah was keenly into research mode. "Well, I am being paid to. Some of this stuff relates to a translation of an almost illegible note on the back of the Piali map, which we haven't been able to make sense of until now. We put it through an image enhancement process. Seb phoned me with the results first thing this morning. It mentions the same characters as that tablet."

He read from his notes. "Nikolas, captain of ships to Iulanos Lord of Athens, hail. The coast from which the enemy fleet sailed is left empty by their ruin. There by your command we have stored and sealed your records, and the memory of Shushannah the Maid of Athens, lest some heir of Osiris should seek once more the dominion of the west. Six stadia by ship from the point, where first our sign is seen.

"Six stadia is just over one kilometre, I remember that from being taught about Jesus' resurrection appearance on the road to Emmaus – the older translations give the distance in stadia," he added as an explanation. "Also the name of St Angelo is scrawled alongside the note."

Bethany was startled by the coincidence with the names. Was there really something worth investigating here? "So what have you found out?"

"About Iulanus and Shushanna, nothing else so far. Except that if Shushanna is the Maid of Athens, that would equate her with Athena, the supposed divine protector of Athens. In that case her sign, and I suppose that of her people, would be the gorgon's head, or a snake from it, according to the mythology. Maybe it refers to some sea monster – there were supposed to be some in the region around Sicily; they were called Scylla and Charybdis, if I remember rightly. Also Athena was a child of Zeus, which would tie in with the other bit of the clue; and she was a virgin, so 'Maid' would be an appropriate term for her. Though this note spells her name with an extra 'h', and Iulanus with an 'o'. Do you think that's significant?"

Bethany wasn't keen on delving into mythology. "The name endings would have to be changed in the Latin tablet, to make the language inflections work. If Shushanna's name really has the 'h' ending, it confirms she was nothing to do with Rome; the name just wouldn't work like that in Latin. As for the other stuff, I'd not put too much weight on that kind of guesswork. What about Brutus, beyond what I said yesterday?"

Josiah indicated the books. "You were mistaken. It's not Brutus as in Caesar's time, but an earlier guy with the same name. In Celtic he would be called Bryttys. Now he is an interesting guy, except for the slight drawback that no one believes he really existed. The story is that he was a great-grandson of the Trojan hero Aeneas, that he was exiled, and that he led a group of Trojans to Britain around 1100 BC. It was this group that founded the pre-Roman kingdoms, which lasted until the Roman conquest. Supposedly the name 'Briton' means 'a follower of Bryttys'. And his grandfather – Aeneas' son – was called Iulus. Also, Lyonesse is an ancient name for Cornwall, probably including parts towards the Scillies that are now under the sea."

Bethany could see a slight problem. "In the New Chronology, Troy fell in the ninth century BC. Around 870, I think. But I wouldn't worry too much about that. The date you've found for Brutus / Bryttys / whoever could be wrong. The chronology is always the difficult bit."

"Maybe your New Chronology has the wrong date for Troy?" suggested Josiah lightly.

Bethany's response was equally light-hearted, but with firm conviction behind it. "If you trust the Bible, then you trust the New Chronology, believe me. Otherwise I shall recommend seven large books and a dozen journals to supplement your reading."

"Okay," said Josiah as they both laughed. He amended some jotted figures. "So that would put Bryttys at around 800 BC, and Iulanus and Shushanna at around 2400 BC." Seeing Bethany react to that, he paused. "What is it?"

Bethany was hesitating between the excitement of a possible discovery, and the alternative possibility that it was just coincidence. "It's very doubtful that the sixteen centuries would be reliable. The problem is – who was counting for all that time? It has to be a summing up by a chronicler who's probably misunderstood some of the details. But just supposing it were reasonably accurate – it's very close to my revision of the date for the Iceman, and therefore to the axe-head and bracelet I found in Cornwall. And the bracelet had the supposed moon-symbol on it. So we might just have confirmed a link between Cornwall and the Mediterranean in the mid-third millennium BC."

"That's brilliant!" exclaimed Josiah enthusiastically.

Bethany had recovered her habitual caution. "No. It's interesting, but purely speculation. It proves nothing on its own. But we need to remember it, in case it starts fitting in with other clues."

Josiah, disappointed but unable to dispute Bethany's expertise, turned to another part of the text. "I've also been thinking about the Zeus reference. Maybe this Iulanus and Shushanna were among the Guardians." He paused in anticipation of a negative reaction, but continued when it didn't come. "I like the idea of a woman helping to attack ships. Sounds like a mermaid. What now?" He'd seen an involuntary flinch.

"Nothing." But her face was betraying something. She sighed. "Well, just don't repeat the mermaid thing, please. It's a family joke that Kath thinks I'm destined to solve a mermaid mystery. But sea kings' fleets..." Now she was back to business. "...if we must go Atlantis hunting, I guess they were the original sea kings. Keep on it."

Professor Mannis glowered at a dossier on his desk. He thrust it towards his assistant, Osgood. "We've got the identity of the woman you described, who was with Hope in Hania."

Bethany's face smiled unconcernedly from a photo. Osgood recognised it and nodded. He looked down the page. "Archaeology graduate. That figures. Christian at... that's the same church as Hope. They must be friends. Well, that makes sense. Lowry couldn't go to Hania for some reason, Hope didn't want to go alone, so he roped in a friend with relevant knowledge."

Mannis cut in. "Except that Hope's brother says that she is part of Lowry's team now."

Osgood wasn't sure how worried he should be. "So Lowry's found someone to compensate for some of the gaps in his own CV. But he knows other archaeologists, like his contact in Hania. What difference does one more make?"

"I'm not sure. But Lowry's never had one actually on his payroll before. She's got negligible real field experience, which will weigh against her, but I don't like the tone of the descriptions we've got."

Osgood checked through them. "She's a member of CHEOPS. The chairman thinks highly of her – that's quite a recommendation. And her tutor says that she breezed through her degree while concentrating on sport. Pretty bright, eh? So she's got brains and contacts. What good are they without information to work on?"

Mannis was still frowning. "Maybe not a lot. But I'm worried about how close Lowry might be to getting significant data. Someone with genuine expertise, albeit raw, might be able to give him a good deal of extra credibility. We've seen that happen before, when the idea that the Sphinx might go back to the time of Osiris got out."

"I thought that had been refuted. The latest research shows that the Sphinx is older than the pyramids, but not by much – maybe a few centuries. A member of CHEOPS would be aware of that." Osgood could see no problem there.

His boss was quick to correct him. "Whoever put that research out didn't stop to consider the implications. The Sphinx relates to a civilization that predates the pyramids; I agree with that. But to stress the shortness of the time gap... I'm surprised the creationists haven't jumped on that. Shortening chronology has a nasty habit of playing into their hands, usually."

Osgood was still relaxed. "Who would take any notice in this case? You almost sound if you were worried that the creationists might be right?" He laughed. Mannis glowered again.

"Still, we're going to need you in Malta now. Lowry's people are moving soon for their 'Treasures of Zeus' hunt. You'll have to stay out of their way, as they know you now, but you will be liaising between me and some local agents. It's imperative that Lowry doesn't find anything further."

There was a knock on the door and a man entered. Vic Osgood found himself being introduced to "my eminent colleague, Doctor Laude, from London".

The latter was carrying a folder with his own copy of the dossiers on Seb, Bethany and Josiah. He came straight to the point. "What beats me is why this Fisher girl should team up with Lowry. It's not even a religious thing; he's no Christian."

Osgood remembered his own job-hunting. "Maybe it's the only offer she got," he suggested. Mannis stared at him, then looked towards Laude.

"It's possible," said Laude. "There are a lot of areas where it's difficult to get graduate work. And her CHEOPS connection would help in some circles but hinder in others; they're quite controversial." An idea was beginning to dawn. "Maybe we could offer her a post?"

"Do we want her?" snapped Mannis. Clearly *he* didn't, at any rate.

"Not as such. But as a way of detaching her from Lowry..." Laude was pondering. He checked the file again. "We have a research post specialising in Latin American antiquities up for grabs. We could offer her that – say that we got a word-of-mouth recommendation, perhaps. That would keep her well away from Malta. And we all know that getting people into the establishment can be a first step in distancing them from controversial views."

"We know which side our bread's buttered," grinned Osgood.

Mannis had finally seen an advantage in the proposal. "At least we upset Lowry's apple-cart. I suppose that compensates for employing a Christian. Okay, it's all right with me if you want to try to headhunt her. But you'd better move fast; Lowry plans to have his people in Malta pretty soon."

"Leave it to me," said Laude. "We'll make her an offer she can't refuse."

10

Blessing

Bethany and Josiah listened with the rest of the congregation, as their pastor recounted their adventure on Crete. "Somehow this seems to be more than a research project. The opposition, and the nature of what they saw, suggests that there's a spiritual issue too. So we're going to pray for them before they head off on the next stage of their quest." Knowing the routine, the pair made their way to the front of the church.

Behind them, Helen stood too. She had been intrigued when Bethany had described what would happen, and had insisted that Seb attend the service with her. He was still sitting, looking bored. "Come on," she urged, "it can't do any harm." Reluctantly, feeling a bit of a fool, the explorer followed his assistants and partner to the front.

The pastor placed his hands on Josiah's shoulders. Three house group leaders came up and did the same for the others; Helen appreciated that it was Josiah's mum who was going to pray for her. They began to pray. Firstly for safe travel and physical well-being, then into the spiritual issues, for the working out of God's purposes and the frustration of the enemy's. Seb started to wonder how long this would last. He shifted his eyes. Clearly his team were into this sort of thing. To his left Josiah, eyes tightly shut, hands open in front of him, wore a rapt expression; as if God were filling those hands to overflowing, filling again and again. And Bethany – he almost fancied a tongue of fire resting on her head, anointing, setting her apart for service. Was this stuff getting to him as well as to Helen now? "Well God," he thought to himself, "if you're really there, and your blessing is on offer, I guess we'd like it." He half-sensed a response, an assurance from outside the physical situation. Then it faded, leaving him wondering if he'd imagined it. Maybe it was waiting for him to lower his wall of scepticism.

The praying ceased. Josiah's friend Carl came forward and asked for the microphone. "Er... I think I may have a word from the Lord for you. I don't know what it means."

"That makes two of us," thought Seb.

"Josiah," continued Carl, "you stand in the place of the guardians."

Josiah and Bethany exchanged glances. "The Guardian from the mountain abides," she quoted.

Josiah stared at the ceiling, musing. "When the sea swallowed its princes," he muttered. The mike caught the words and amplified them to the room. Josiah realised an explanation was called for. "That's from a clue Mr Lowry found. We figured the sea princes as Atlantis – the kingdom of Atlas. The Guardian survived when Atlas fell – or was judged. 'The children of Zeus fought against Atlas' – perhaps they were the good guys in this picture. I said there were some." He looked at his teammates as he finished.

"Zeus – a pagan god and a good guy?" The man who had been praying for Seb could not swallow that.

Seb smiled. Now he could brush away some blindness induced by religious preconceptions. "Not Zeus the god, but Zeus the human being behind the myths. Behind those stories are real people from the depths of history, ordinary people like us. Why shouldn't some of them be good people?"

Bethany was nodding agreement. "This whole thing is delving into realms that we know of more from mythology than science. The thing we are going to look for is described as the 'Treasures of Zeus', and as being 'hidden from the eyes of Osiris'. That puts Zeus and Osiris on opposite sides. Now Osiris is also Orion, the hunter in the sky, sometimes shortened to On. There's a priest of On mentioned in the story of Joseph in Egypt. But the hunter figure has also been identified with an early Mesopotamian king called Enmer-Kar. The 'Kar' bit means 'hunter'. The 'Enmer' bit is thought to be the Biblical Nimrod. 'Enmer-Kar' equals 'Nimrod the hunter'." She paused as she sensed that the audience were struggling to follow this. "Look, sorry for all the academic stuff, but trust me, okay? Please? Nimrod was evil, the great rebel of Babel. If Osiris was also Orion the hunter, then behind the myth of Osiris may lurk the reality of Nimrod. And if Zeus was on the other side, we might guess that he was someone trying to be true to God, like Abraham was." She glanced towards Josiah as another thought struck her. "Maybe he was one preserving the memory of the covenant with Noah."

"But Zeus got up to all kinds of immorality." There was a murmur of agreement with that comment, made by the same house group leader who had prayed for Seb.

"Well," replied Bethany, "I never said that he was perfect. But in any case the myths have been garbled over many centuries. The Zeus who fought against Atlas may originally have been a totally different character from Zeus the adulterer, but then they became combined as the tales were re-told down the generations."

"So Zeus is two people, but Osiris and Nimrod are one person?" The house group leader was mentally notching up debating points for his side of the argument.

Bethany frowned. "Perhaps. Who knows?"

"No," intervened Seb firmly. "Osiris was also portrayed as the judge who weighed the spirits of the dead, and admitted the good to heaven. That sounds closer to your God than to Nimrod, the rebel against the will of heaven. You can't say that A, B and C in myths are always X, Y and Z respectively in history. All we're doing is looking at one story and saying that here, say, Osiris looks like Nimrod, and Zeus looks like Noah, or someone upholding his memory. In the next story it could be completely different. The true history has been garbled over millennia."

Bethany agreed, but could see that many others present were unconvinced. She tried another tack. "Look, you've backed me through three years of study and several years of growing in faith.

I'm not going to suddenly turn round and endorse something that's contrary to the Bible, and neither is Josiah. All we've just been talking about is speculation. Wait for our conclusions, we won't let you down."

The pastor smiled. "I think there's wisdom in that. Bethany's studies are among many things that I don't fully understand. But her gift is from God, and it will bear fruit in his time." He paused. "Let's move on."

"Now this is really odd timing." Bethany sat at the breakfast table, holding a letter. "I was finally sure that this thing with Seb was in line with God's will for me. Now I get an offer from a top London college: 'Come and see if your CHEOPS ideas will hold up in Peru … We want the best and we've heard that you're in that category. Show up on Thursday and prove it to us, and the job's yours.' Now what do I do?"

"Recognition at last," smiled her sister Kath. "It's about time that your CHEOPS friends pulled some strings for you."

"But is it right?" persisted Bethany. "If it is, why did God seem to set up this thing with Seb, so that I would sign up for it?"

"Maybe to deal with your discouragement at getting nowhere," suggested Kath. "Surely you can go along to the interview and check it out, without having to make a decision there and then?"

Bethany agreed, still uncertain.

Bethany had sat through a hard sell by Doctor Laude. She knew of his name and work through references in various CHEOPS papers. Although Laude had never endorsed the key theories being advanced by CHEOPS, his work in Peru and Ecuador was so important that other researchers could not ignore it. Ironically, he was selling her a similar line to the one Seb had used, giving her scope to develop her own views and put them to the test against colleagues who differed. Colleagues, that was, if she took the job.

She was still unsure, and she was praying silently about it even as the interview proceeded. The superb London facilities were a major attraction for her, and the money was good. Only a matter of days ago she would have accepted without hesitation. But after all that she had been through, was it right to change course now?

Laude was drawing his pitch to a close. "Unfortunately we need a quick decision. We had another candidate lined up before we heard of you, and the project wheels are already in motion. In fact, we would be extremely happy if you were to sign here and now."

Bethany thought it over. It occurred to her that she should check out whether this haste was really necessary. "The timing is a bit awkward for me. I've committed to some... er, freelance work in the next few weeks. It would be really helpful if you could give me a little while to think about it. And to work my notice," she invented as an afterthought.

Laude seemed very anxious about this. "Freelance work?" he asked.

"Yes, well, it's a little more formal than that. I'm heading out to Malta with – would you believe..." she grinned in embarrassed fashion "...*Seb Lowry*, the author of Ancient Quest. Just to keep my hand in until some proper work comes along, of course. But having made that commitment, I'd like to be able to keep to it before joining you."

"But surely there's no comparison between working with us and working with the matchstick civilizations man?"

This was a surprisingly sharp reply. Had she hit a nerve? She resolved to spin the line a bit further. "Of course there isn't. I've been dreaming of facilities like you have here. But one of the features you mentioned that I'd been recommended for is integrity. I've given Lowry my word, and I'd like to keep it."

Laude could not believe this. His tone began to sharpen. "Ms Fisher, er... Bethany," – he was recovering his smoothness – "you must realise that an association with Lowry will only damage your professional credibility. It will make it more difficult for me to convince my bosses that you are the right person for this post. I

85

really feel that I should insist – with your own interests in mind as well – that you choose now: Lowry or us."

"Right now?" Bethany was getting increasingly suspicious. "Don't I even get to go home and think it over?"

Laude was still amazed and making no attempt to hide it. "Think it over? I realize that's usual practice with job offers, but surely this is a special case, one where the right move is obvious?" He decided to push harder. "If you even think Lowry is a credible alternative, I may have to withdraw this offer."

Bethany realized that a further ploy was needed. She thought quickly and came up with something. "Who says that you and Lowry are my only alternatives here? At least give me the weekend. I'll ring up Monday, maybe even tomorrow, if I decide to accept."

Laude noted the implication of a third option, wondered who it might be and whether he should let her take it up. It could hardly be worse than Lowry, from his viewpoint. He tried to find out. "Who else is after you? Are they offering more money? We may be able to move on that."

Bethany smiled. "Let's just say that I have some options, which each have their attractions. I promise you a quick decision."

Reluctantly, Laude agreed.

Back home, Bethany was soon in contact with Seb Lowry. "They were really putting on the pressure; I could hardly believe it. I had to invent another job offer, merely to get out of there without signing a contract on the spot."

Seb was surprised. "Haven't you taken the London job then? It sounds like all that you ever wanted."

"It is. Two or three weeks ago, I would have gone for it at once. But since the Crete trip, and that service last Sunday week, I've been pretty sure that working with you is the right thing to do. In line with God's will, if you'll excuse the concept. That would make the alternative a temptation, something to be avoided. One thing that occurred to me: we talked about a cover-up once. It seems to me that this just might be more of it – we might be getting close to something, so they're trying to distract me away from it."

"I don't know," said Seb slowly, considering. "If you grant the assumption that something is being covered up, it fits the pattern. Well, I'd be delighted to keep you on my team, but I'll understand if you feel that you have to grab this opportunity."

Bethany did take the weekend to think about it. In the end she decided that a faith decision was needed. She wrote Doctor Laude a courteous letter, regretting that prior commitments prevented her from accepting his offer at this time.

"She turned me down!" Laude was incredulous. "And she refers to prior commitments, not an alternative offer. That means she's sticking with Lowry. The girl's a nutcase."

Mannis was forced to hold the phone away from his ear, Laude was so loud. "Unfortunately, there is another possibility. Lowry and Fisher may be closer to the truth than we thought. Our contact got a hint that Lowry may actually have possession of the bracelet and axe-head from Cornwall. Thinking back, he did seem unconcerned at someone making off with it. I don't know how he could have arranged to intercept me at that park, but it looks like he did."

Laude could see that this made sense. The prospect of a major discovery – if she really understood how huge it could be – would be sufficient to keep Bethany on Lowry's team. "That must be a big worry. Can we keep them from getting to Malta?"

"Afraid not. Free movement of people is one of the selling points for our super-state, at least for the moment. But I already have arrangements in hand to monitor them very carefully once they get there."

11

Journey

The team were back at Josiah's family home for a pre-flight get-together, and Seb was filling everyone in on how the preparations were going. "Actually, I'm regretting recruiting you," he quipped. "It's all the extra expenses: two more flight tickets, three hotel rooms instead of one, insurance in case you sue me..."

Bethany broke in, sounding irritated. "In case we sue you?"

"Well, yes," came the answer, "you can't be too careful nowadays." Seb was wondering how he'd upset Bethany this time.

She explained. "Look, I know we have our differences, but I have signed up and I'm a team player." The snappiness creeping into her voice threatened to contradict the last remark.

Seb tried to calm things down. "Yes, but, say you break a leg, you might want damages from me."

Bethany sighed. "A few years ago my church wanted to put on a big outreach event. We found we couldn't afford it precisely because of this insurance and compensation business. Some of us got to thinking that there's a need for churches to be counter-cultural on this sort of thing – that as Christians we shouldn't go after compensation unless there's clear evidence of an attempt to harm us. It's like what St Paul explained to the Corinthian church – we always have the right to *not* assert our rights. Living the Kingdom way is more important."

"The Kingdom way?" queried Seb.

"Sorry, that's jargon. Living in a way appropriate to being under God's rule."

Across the room, Paul Hope was smiling. "God's Kingdom is about seeing things differently. That's what makes it great for people with autism – we're already used to seeing the world differently."

The conversation turned to plans for the expedition. Josiah's family were keen to know all about it, and Seb was happy to oblige, provided that they kept their knowledge to themselves. He was convinced that Mannis or people like him would try to obstruct him if they found out what he was doing. "We'll only tell a few prayer supporters," came the assurance.

Seb's questioning look invited clarification. "Don't worry," said Josiah. "Anything covered in a prayer gathering at our church will be treated as confidential, not to be discussed outside the meeting."

So Seb expounded his plans. He was convinced that the sixteenth century Turkish attack on Malta, with Piali's map at their disposal, had the Treasures of Zeus as a key objective. The attackers' full weight had been thrown first against Fort St Elmo, on the tip of the peninsula where Valletta was subsequently built, and then against the Knights' headquarters across the harbour in Birgu. It didn't deter him that historians had attributed other motives to their strategy; after all, the historians had not seen Piali's map. That the name of one of the Knights' strongholds had been written on the back of the map confirmed his thinking. "They must have had good reason to believe that what they wanted was there."

Bethany had been reading up on the history, and had an objection ready. "But they took St Elmo and didn't find the Treasures of Zeus."

Seb had to acknowledge this. "True. So then they went for Birgu and Senglea. They could have just penned the Knights in their fortresses and searched anywhere else that took their fancy. They must have thought that the Knights were hoarding the treasure," he reiterated.

Mr Hope asked whether, in that case, the Knights had themselves found the treasure.

Seb didn't think so. "There's no record of it. If they did, it's probably gone for ever by now – stolen by Napoleon's French expedition and then sunk by Nelson at the Battle of the Nile. If they knew – and intended to look – they changed their priorities after the Great Siege. All their energy went into building Valletta and bolstering the rest of the defences. But I've finally got permission to do some scans around the forts – use some ground-penetrating radar and see if any anomalies show up. If I find anything, we'll have more ammunition to request permission to dig."

"I still think that we should try other places too," put in Josiah. "The Turks may have misunderstood the clues. There's nothing about them that we're sure relates only to the forts. I'd vote for Gozo. A snake carving was found there once, at the prehistoric temples of Ggantija. It's the right general era, and the snake was Athena's emblem. That ties in with our clues."

Seb was not convinced. He got out a map and pointed out that Ggantija was too far inland. "The clues refer to six stadia and the coast. But yes, we could plot the distance from the temples, say along their sunrise alignments, and see what's in that area."

Bethany had looked up from her plate at the mention of the snake carving. "There was another snake carving found just last year," she said. "At the Tarxien temples. It's new and I've only just found out about it," she added, noting surprise all round the table.

Seb grabbed a map, and Bethany reached across to locate the site for him. He checked the scale. "No more than one kilometre, say about five stadia, from the nearest part of Grand Harbour. I'd say that strengthens the case for looking in Fort St Angelo in Birgu."

Bethany had another item for the agenda. "I've done a bit of work on the details of that map you showed us in Portsmouth." Seb looked her way, expecting another argument. But his expression invited her to continue. "The first thing I noticed was that the latitude scales on each edge don't align. Horizontal is not east-west, but rotated eleven and a quarter degrees anticlockwise."

Josiah broke in, amazed. "How can you be that precise about the angle?"

Bethany grinned. "There are thirty-two points on the compasses on the map, aren't there? Eleven and a quarter degrees is one thirty-second of a circle – one compass point."

"That's a feature of the map design type," put in Seb. "Analysis of the Piri Re'is map suggested that one of the component parts was rotated by something like seven compass points."

Bethany continued. "On the western edge, the latitudes seem to check out pretty well, once you draw them with that eleven and a quarter degree slant; at least within the bit below fifty degrees or so north – further north the map becomes unrecognisable. Which just happens to be the same point where your Piali map stops. You might be right that further north couldn't be mapped as it was glaciated. But on the eastern side the latitudes get further out. The Black Sea, although it looks pretty much the right shape, is drawn too far north and too large. I also get the impression that the longitudes aren't that precise. Not too far out by eye, and better than on the average medieval map, but not accurate when measured. I haven't found a pattern to the errors." She paused.

"Any conclusions?" asked Seb.

"Not really," she replied. "There could be a history of miscopying, misaligning scales, as has been suggested for other ancient maps. But I don't like to speculate on that; there's no way it can be proven. Actually, my hunch is that it confirms your general thinking." Seb raised his eyebrows. Bethany expanded her point. "A really advanced civilization would have had chronometers and accurate measurements. I think it looks more like the outcome of using a good but approximate system of measurement; the sort of thing that might be expected if the people of the stone circles era had some genuine astronomical knowledge, but not a really high civilisation."

"But the astronomical knowledge required would be advanced, wouldn't it?" put in Josiah. Seb nodded.

Bethany hesitated. "Yes, well, that's true, I guess. It's another layer of mystery. Advanced knowledge, but not so advanced technology. Let's hope we find something on Malta to resolve things."

Josiah always preferred the window seat when flying. He had watched the steep and steady climb from Gatwick out over the Channel, which previously he'd only done at night or in cloudy conditions. He had followed the flight path across France, past the western end of the Alps, and out over the Mediterranean. Now he could see the wing configuration changing, the rear panels clawing at the air instead of allowing it to stream past. They were beginning to descend. On the port quarter, a distant plume of ash marked the location of Etna, once again active. Ahead, across miles of water, was one tiny speck of land where their hopes and dreams would stand or fall.

Beside Josiah, Bethany sat absorbed in a book. Ever the professional, even in casual travelling clothes, she was revising her knowledge of early Maltese history in preparation for their task. For a moment as he glanced at her, Josiah's respect for a Christian and a colleague gave way to other thoughts about the attractive woman at his side. But there was no spark there. Four years his senior, armed with an intellect that few could match, she was never going to be the woman of his dreams. Now, the girl he'd seen an hour or so earlier, making her way up the aisle – that was someone worth a dream. Maybe West Indian or perhaps Latin American, even a mixture of both, she had a poise and a figure worth watching. Just maybe they were heading for the same resort...

Josiah emerged from his thoughts to find the ground rising to meet the plane. Expertly handled, it dropped to earth with the merest suggestion of a jolt. The brakes came on and they slowed smoothly to taxiing speed. They were in Malta.

Seb grabbed his bag from the locker, keyed up, impatient for action, ready to go. When travelling alone, he would take an aisle seat and was usually among the first off the plane. Now he chose to stay with his charges. Helen, used to being hustled by him, was ready with her bag in hand. Less practised, Bethany and Josiah took longer to retrieve their things and push out into the corridor. They queued for passport control and then went through to reclaim their suitcases and the expedition gear.

While they watched the conveyor belt for the last items, a vaguely familiar voice sounded behind them. "Miss Fisher, Mr Hope. What are you smuggling this time?" Behind them was the security official whom they had met on their return from Crete. They turned sharply and saw a smiling traveller in casual clothes. There was no seriousness to the challenge. "Garfield Pentecost, pleased to see you again," he continued. "My wife Elizabeth, our teenagers, Nerys and Reggie." To Josiah's delight, he indicated the girl he had noticed earlier, standing a few yards away watching over some bags.

"Hi," he responded, wanting a conversation to start. "Er..." gesturing towards Seb, "I would like to declare a mad Atlantis hunter. Oh, and Bethany is hiding a supercomputer inside her head." She gave her customary glare at the unappreciated humour. "Sorry, sense of humour malfunction. Joke?" said Josiah quickly.

Bethany's gaze softened fractionally as she decided to let the irritation pass.

"We're heading for Sliema. What about you?" asked Josiah hopefully.

"So are we," said Mr Pentecost. He named a hotel which wasn't the same as the one Seb had booked.

"Oh well, might see you around anyway." Josiah would gladly have arranged to meet, but at that moment the last bag appeared.

Seb had a trolley full, all set to move. He shepherded his group away. "No offence, but we aren't on a tourist trip. We have a job to do. Goodbye."

Josiah cast a couple of glances behind him as he followed Seb and the others out of the airport.

12

Malta

Valletta, capital of Malta, is built on a peninsula in the middle of a vast bay. It does not jut out beyond the general trend of the coastline, but divides the water either side into the two huge basins of Marsamxett and Grand Harbour. At the time of the great siege, the Knights had fortified only the tip of the peninsula and parts of the eastern side of Grand Harbour. Following the victory, they had built their new fortress capital with haste but also strict planning. It was named after their victorious Grand Master, who lies buried beneath its cathedral. Seb would have liked to take rooms in Valletta, but the budget was tight and Sliema was cheaper.

Seb took the group to a high vantage point looking out across Grand Harbour, with a good prospect of his intended target, Fort St Angelo. From the eastern ramparts, they looked out over Grand Harbour and saw Fort St Angelo below them across the water. He could imagine the Turkish commanders standing on that very spot, discussing plans to search out the fort. Josiah too imagined the scene in 1565, with cannon balls flying both ways across the intervening water. Seb also tried to picture the place millennia earlier, wondering where an ancient king might choose to hide his precious relics. Soon, he hoped, he would have the answer.

Seb had holidayed on Malta before, many years ago. He had a fair idea of the geography in his head. He had arranged a car rental – though the car had to stay outside the crowded, largely pedestrianised capital city in a designated car park – and wanted to acquaint his team with the harbour layout. They then drove back round the western bay to Sliema, where they were based, to join a harbour cruise.

Waiting among a group of tourists, Seb idly flicked through a brochure. Something caught his eye. "Any of you fancy a round island cruise later? It's on me if our search is successful." His team, who were absorbed in scanning the harbour, didn't respond.

They walked up the gangplank for the harbour trip. Helen shivered slightly in the onshore breeze and would have made for the sheltered lower deck, but Josiah was before her and already climbing on to the upper deck, in the hope of better photographs. The others followed him. Soon their trip was under way, starting anticlockwise around Marsamxett – the western harbour – and making its way under the great walls and earthworks which still defend Valletta. Josiah took numerous pictures, concentrating particularly on Fort St Elmo at the tip of the peninsula, where the walls and buildings dipped to the sea. This was a pre-siege stronghold of the Knights, gallantly defended until all were overwhelmed, and so a possible target for their search.

Beyond Fort St Elmo, in the short stretch between the two harbours, they suddenly caught the Mediterranean swell. Josiah almost lost his footing as he tried for a last photograph of the fort. Hastily he rejoined his friends at their seats. Helen pulled a pullover tighter around herself, against the wind.

The swell dropped abruptly as they cleared the breakwater at the mouth of Grand Harbour. Josiah made haste to reclaim standing room, along with the other tourist photographers, as they came under the eastern flank of Valletta. Bethany also took a few snaps, though her camera was mainly for work. The boat continued past a docked cruise liner, eventually reaching the eastern half of Grand Harbour. Here two promontories stuck out side by side, pointing towards Valletta: Senglea and Vittorioso, the latter also known as Birgu, but renamed in honour of victory against the Turks. At the tip of Vittorioso, a ditch all but turned its point into an island, isolating the stronghold of Fort St Angelo. Seb gazed at the colours of the Knights, which still flew alongside the flag of Malta. This was the spot on which his hopes were chiefly resting. He imagined himself inside the fort, digging, digging – finding... who knows what?

Then they were past the fort, heading back to the western harbour and soon returning to dry land.

"There!" shouted Josiah. Seb brought the hired car to a sudden stop. After several minutes of wandering up and down side streets, they had finally located the Tarxien Temples, where the more recent of the two snake carvings had been found. They parked, paid a small entrance fee, and emerged into an open space containing several exposed megalithic structures. The bell of the next-door church of Santa Teresa pealed the hour.

No guidebook was available, but Bethany pulled a set of notes from her backpack and led the way into the complex. Reaching a trilithon structure, still intact or else restored, she turned left through it into the temple, intent on reaching the inner sanctum where the discovery had been made.

But in the second chamber Seb stopped short. Bethany realized he was no longer following her, and came back to see why. Various carved stones lay around on both sides of the passage, the carvings still clearly visible on many of them. But what had arrested Seb's attention were the barely visible marks on two upright standing stones, which were highlighted on the information board for visitors. Bethany looked, and she too sucked in her breath. Her mind flew to memories of Egypt's Eastern Desert.

Josiah was unsure what was significant. "What is it?" he asked.

Seb pointed to the reproduced drawings on the board. "These ships. Note the high prow and stern – the best example is this fainter one here. These are not the wooden rafts that tourists probably get told about. These are reed boats like Thor Heyerdahl made."

Josiah was confused. "But Heyerdahl's Kon Tiki was a wooden raft."

"Yes, but his later trips used reed boats: Ra 1, Ra 2 and Tigris, sailing across the Atlantic and then around the Indian Ocean. I've not seen reed boats mentioned in connection with Malta, but it doesn't surprise me to find them. It's entirely typical for a seagoing culture of that era. And it shows a connection with the Middle East, probably Mesopotamia, where Heyerdahl had Tigris built."

"They're found in Egypt too," added Bethany. "I've seen drawings just like these, from the Egyptian end of the sea route round Arabia from the Persian Gulf. And in Sweden. The Swedish versions are associated with similar Bronze Age work, but" – thinking it through as she spoke – "it would make sense if the stone carvings were earlier, before bronze was available."

Seb gave her a funny look. "Are you agreeing with me?"

Bethany grinned. "Yes. It's funny what can happen when you get things right."

"So," said Seb, "who says that Malta's culture developed in isolation now? Never trust what they tell the tourists. This would be the work of the same people who drew the original Mediterranean portolan map. The first stone structures, or even temporary wooden ones to start with, would have been for surveying purposes – the sort of stone circle you can find in various parts of Western Europe."

By now Bethany was frowning. It seemed that their agreement was a fragile, temporary truce.

"You disagree?"

"Once again, it's pure speculation," she asserted.

"But you admitted, when I showed you the portolan, that you didn't know who else could have drawn it."

Bethany had to concede that much. "That's true. But it doesn't mean I have to accept the first possible explanation that comes along. I'm waiting for positive evidence to support it."

Seb was exasperated. "The well-known temple solar alignments, the… the mere fact that they could navigate well enough to find this little speck of an island. What more do you want? It has to be a strong possibility."

She nodded. "A possibility. Nothing more, so far. Against it is the improbability that such an early society could have the required scientific knowledge."

"Are you denying the astronomical alignments?" asked Seb incredulously.

"Of course not," said Bethany, her patience beginning to be tested. "But they are simple observation, trial and error. Plotting a map is clever science. You can't go straight from one to the other." Then, realizing that this was coming over as far too negative, "Look, you're paying me to point out the objections, show you where you need more evidence. That's all I'm doing."

As the last point sunk in, Seb's frustration subsided. "Okay. I just wish you could tell me what evidence you would accept."

"Who knows? You can only find what's there to be found. How could I specify that in advance?"

After that, the spot where the snake carving had been unearthed was an anticlimax. Nothing remained on site except a notice, and a hole to mark the spot. They took some photographs and had a look around. Soon they were in the car again, heading back to Sliema.

The next morning, Seb angrily flung an envelope on the breakfast table. "They've rescinded permission for the radar scans," he shouted furiously. "I've gone to all the expense of hiring the gear and shipping it out here, and now they won't let us use it."

Bethany hurriedly scanned the letter between mouthfuls of muesli. "I presume we can appeal?"

Seb was not mollified. "I'm sure we can. But it took me weeks to get permission in the first place. I'm paying a fortune every week for the radar. I can't afford to have it sitting idle. Plus the extra hotel bills for a longer stay." A waiter raised an eyebrow as he removed some empty dishes. "Even though it's a good hotel," appended Seb.

He continued in this vein through the meal. By the end of breakfast, he was all set to go to the forts and survey them unofficially. "We can sneak the radar machine in in a backpack; it's small enough."

Bethany tried to caution him against that. Her instincts were to stay within the rules, both as a Christian and as an archaeologist. Breaking a government restriction would be yet another blot on her CV. As for how Seb could fund the delay, she sympathised but had no answer. She had not concerned herself with the details of the budget, but clearly money was tight.

Tiring of the argument, Bethany was first to leave the table. Seb continued to talk to Josiah and Helen. Bringing two assistants was a serious drain on his funding, which in any case depended ultimately on unknown future revenue from books and television. He simply could not afford to wait around. In the end he resolved to walk into the fort and challenge someone to stop him. "Will you come with me?"

Helen didn't answer. She was not there for the field trips; the question was not addressed to her.

Josiah pondered the dilemma. "Like you, I don't see what other choice we have. But please leave Bethany out of it, I can see her point; she doesn't want a reputation as a law-breaker. We can't go today anyway if we're posing as tourists. My guidebook says that the forts are only open at weekends."

So it came about that Seb and Josiah travelled round the bay to Fort St Angelo the following Saturday. It was a sunny day, with some light cloud but no prospect of rain, warm but not oppressively hot.

Seb parked near the entrance to the dock of the old town of Birgu. "I came here once as a tourist, years ago. Got lost trying to find the fort. Past the wharf and the Maritime Museum is the only way in. All the side-streets lead to dead ends."

They walked along the waterfront and over a bridge. The fort was separated from the peninsula by a water-filled ditch, which dated from the time of the Knights. On the way up to the fort entrance they passed a notice, forbidding cars except on official business. But there were no 'keep out' signs. Now and again they nodded greetings to other visitors coming down, as they climbed the paths into the fort's interior. They expected a ticket office and an admission charge, but found none.

At length they emerged on to an open space between the old walls. Josiah walked to a room and peered through the empty doorway into the dim interior. "Where's the way down?" he asked.

"Down?" queried Seb.

"To the underground store rooms, or dungeons, or whatever," explained Josiah.

"As far as I know, there aren't any," said Seb. "Everything below us is rock – unless there is something hidden – but a hidden chamber is what I expect to find." He took the small radar unit from his backpack and placed it on the ground, fixing its antennae. Then he chose a spot, apparently at random. Starting from a wall, he took four paces into the courtyard, towing the machine behind him. At his request, Josiah photographed the spot for reference, taking care to include fixed points in the background.

Seb activated the machine. An unseen radar pulse fired into the ground. He paused while the on-board storage system digested the results, then took another pace forward and repeated the procedure. Then another pace, scanning a line across the fort. The next stage would be a parallel line alongside the first one.

He had paced back and forth several times when suddenly two men in uniform entered the courtyard. "Mr Lowry?" asked one.

Seb was alarmed, but pretended nonchalance. "Yes – at your service." Josiah felt his heart start to beat fast.

"You do not have permission for this device," said one policeman.

Seb feigned ignorance. "Yes I do. I arranged it all before coming to Malta." He produced an official letter from the responsible ministry. The countermanding letter had conveniently been left behind.

The policeman looked over the letter. One spoke into his radio in Maltese. An answer came back. Then the man addressed Seb. "This permission has been revoked. A letter was sent to your hotel."

Seb acted innocent. "A letter? What letter? I don't know what you're talking about." Josiah tried to stay calm, at least outwardly.

The policemen conferred in their own language. "Very well. Perhaps this is a mistake. But you are no longer allowed to use your machine here. We will confiscate it."

Seb tried to object. "You have no right. I have permission for this." He snatched the device up.

Again the policemen conferred. "You will leave here. Now."

It was useless to object. Seb and Josiah allowed themselves to be shepherded out of the fort. At the entrance was a police car. Again the men demanded custody of the radar device. Again Seb objected, but he was forced to back down, despite threatening to take his complaint as high as necessary. At least, during the walk out of the fort, he had managed to remove and palm the disk on which the morning's data was stored.

The policemen drove off. Seb and Josiah retreated to their own car and returned to base.

Bethany burst in on Seb's review of his radar data. She had just heard of the events at Fort St Angelo, and she was seething.

Seb tried to explain. "Bethany. I have a tight budget. I can't afford to wait."

"Well, now you have no choice, with your equipment confiscated. Look, you may be able to tread on toes, but this could damage me. Archaeologists are supposed to work within the law."

Seb tried to repair the damage. "Why do you think I left you here?" he asked quietly. "I have logged... er, that is *will* log... your objection. I will make clear to anyone who asks that you were not party to today's venture. But please try to understand the constraints I'm working under."

Bethany thought it over. Slowly her anger dissipated. "Okay. Thanks for leaving me out of it. But please try not to do anything like that again." Then she grinned. "I'd better not show an interest. But you might care to volunteer any results you obtained."

Seb gestured at the featureless screen. "All negative. We only covered a very small fraction of the site, but so far we've drawn a blank."

By dinner, Seb had reflected on the events of the morning. "Who knew where we were going?" he asked. The others looked up questioningly from their plates. "How did the police know what we were doing and where? Someone tipped them off."

None of the others liked the implication. Bethany immediately deployed her ironclad alibi. "You can't blame me. I didn't know anything about it."

Seb nodded. "Helen?"

She appreciated the question even less than Bethany. "Of course I wouldn't tell anyone," she snapped.

That left Josiah. "No, I didn't tell anyone." Then he reflected. "Oh, just my brother. Just for the prayer meeting I told you about. Church people. Our plans wouldn't go outside that meeting."

"Only your church?" queried Seb.

"Yes," then realising he was wrong again, "and a fellow-Christian he plays chess with."

Seb's gaze focussed on him at once. "Who?"

"I don't know. What does it matter?"

"It matters because they passed on what you told them," snapped Seb.

"Rubbish," retorted Josiah.

The discussion degenerated to "yes they did, no they didn't".

Helen interrupted, if only to shut them up. "Why not check it out?" Both Seb and Josiah looked at her. Helen tried to spin out her spur of the moment thought. "Plant some false information; say that you're going to break another restriction. Then see if anyone acts on it."

As they thought about it, it began to make sense. "Josiah," said Seb slowly, "please tell your brother that we intend to join a scuba trip; mingling with tourists diving off Comino, where we think we may find ancient remains." Josiah nodded.

The tour operator was nonplussed. "I'm very sorry, but this is out of my control. I cannot take you diving off Comino today." Several disgruntled tourists departed unwillingly, muttering to themselves.

Across the road, Seb and Helen sat eating ice creams, watching what was happening. Evidently there really was someone out to stop their research.

13

Look to the East

Vic Osgood was in an upbeat mood. He had just conferred with his bosses in England, and everyone was pleased with progress so far. Seb Lowry's team had been stopped from investigating Fort St Angelo, and prevented from reaching Comino altogether. Their mole in the camp reported that the prayer news was that money was running low, and inspiration for how to continue the search was lacking.

The prayer support group was indeed about to meet in a special session. Josiah's brother Paul, Bethany's sister Kate, Carl – back from university for a visit home – and several of their friends were present. So was Paul's chess-playing friend, George, who had initially been reluctant to attend, but who had allowed Paul to persuade him of the importance of the meeting. That was the version for Paul. In reality, he had conferred with Mannis to decide whether he should show up. It was a case of balancing the desire for information against the possibility that he would sound so out of place that he would arouse suspicion. After all, he was an infrequent churchgoer, and never went to prayer meetings. Regular churchgoers weren't the sort of person that Mannis could easily find among his preferred acquaintances.

The meeting focussed in part on the loss of the radar device, and the consequent financial issues. Kate, naturally, prayed principally for Bethany; Paul for Josiah. Carl wasn't sure what to ask for. He let his thoughts ramble, and recollected the pastor's reference to a spiritual battle. In his heart, rather than out loud, he prayed for discernment and protection.

One by one, each person present joined in. George realized that he would have to say something; it would be less conspicuous than being the only one to say nothing. He waited for a gap in the flow of prayers, and came in with some pious sounding words which he hoped would be taken as being his accustomed style of praying. As he finished, Paul added a loud "Amen!" and other members of the group murmured assent.

Carl sat silent. He was trying not to judge the style of prayer, but something about the substance of it did not ring true. He opened his mouth to pray again. "Lord, we've been told that there seem to be spiritual issues here, obstructing the research. We don't know what's going on behind the scenes, but we pray that you will defeat the enemy's schemes. Please give Bethany and Josiah a breakthrough; let them find what you have sent them to discover."

After the meeting, Carl walked home with Paul and Kate. "Josiah was right," he said. "That man George is not what he seems to be. I just feel it somehow."

"Bethany mentioned that she seemed to have run into some sort of cover-up in Cornwall," recalled her sister. "And then there was that business on Crete; someone tried to pinch the relic they went to see."

"Not just anyone," put in Paul. "It was the man Josiah had seen in Italy, one of the assistants of Seb Lowry's bete-noire Mannis."

"But we don't see anything that would justify a cover-up," said Kate. "There must be something they haven't found, but which that fellow Mannis knows they're getting close to. Something important. But what?"

They walked on in silence for a bit, thoughts churning away but going nowhere fast. Soon they came to the Hope's home. Paul wondered about asking them in, but his habitual shyness came over him and he didn't find the words. It always happened to him when a girl was around. He walked up the path alone, let himself in, cursing inwardly at the social gaucheness which came with his condition. Suddenly a distracting thought struck him. He welcomed the change of mood, then gasped as it took shape. Suppose the thing his brother was searching for had a bearing on the truth of the Bible? That would surely bring spiritual forces into the action. Galvanised by the idea, he went straight to his room and sat down to pray some more. Sometimes he found his relationship with God difficult – like every other relationship was for him – but not tonight. He was praying for God to move in power, and he could feel an answer in his spirit. Something was happening somewhere.

Bethany sat at the breakfast table, examining an email which had arrived overnight. The regular CHEOPS mailshot had news from research around the globe, principally from Egypt, but near the end of this month's bulletin was a reference to a dig in Malta. A derelict hotel in Marsascala at the eastern end of the island was being made safe and prepared for redevelopment, but some archaeologists were being allowed to investigate the area at the same time. She decided to pay a visit, having nothing else to do that was directly related to Seb's project.

Seb agreed it was a worthwhile move. He offered to drive her, but Bethany was adamant that she would make a better impression if she arrived on her own. Seb reluctantly accepted that his dubious reputation would count against him here. Instead, he helped Bethany to identify the bus route to use. It's said that all roads lead to Rome; in Malta, all buses lead to Valletta. So it was a case of catching any bus heading out of Sliema, and then finding the one to carry on eastwards.

"I'll try to think of something for Josiah and me to do while you're gone," said Seb.

"Where is Josiah anyway?" Bethany hadn't seen him that morning. In fact he had risen early and gone for a fairly random walk through Sliema. He had a mixture of motives for getting away: frustration at the events at Fort St Angelo; a vague feeling that he didn't have enough expertise to help much; lack of company – neither the intellectual Bethany nor the older Helen were natural friends for him. With no immediate work to take his mind off things, he gave in to a memory that was playing in the back of his mind.

Down at the waterside, a dark-skinned teenage woman paused to take in the view. Josiah spotted her and his heart skipped a beat. Swiftly he moved towards her. "Nerys, hi!" Startled, she looked round, blankly. "We almost met at the airport. Your dad spoke to me. My name's Josiah."

Slowly a memory surfaced. She laughed, partly out of relief that the stranger accosting her at least shared her faith. "Oh. The Christian terrorist, Josiah. Named after the last of the good kings of Judah; child of a generation marked for doom, for the sins of their fathers. It is a good name for someone living today – who might see the Tribulation and Rapture."

Josiah agreed. Both he and his brother liked the Bible story of King Josiah as a model of faithful witness in the face of impending and imminent doom.

"So, what brings you here?" asked Nerys.

"Just taking some time off," said Josiah.

"Oh yes, you're not here on holiday, are you?"

Soon Josiah was telling the reason why he was in Malta, over coffee in a harbour-side café. Nerys, out on a walk to get some space from her family, was happy to accept the company of someone her own age. Josiah threw in all the details of the last few months, wanting to keep the conversation going as long as possible. The terrorism frame-up proved a popular episode, Nerys laughing heartily at her dad's confusion.

"Do you expect to get another shot at searching the fort?" she queried when Josiah had finally finished.

"I don't know. We hope so. It's about the right distance from where the snake carving was found – six stadia, which is just over one kilometre in modern terms. And as I said, the snake was Athena's emblem. So the clues seem to point there."

Nerys pondered. "But didn't you say that you had another name for Athena?"

"I think so. 'Shushanna of the mountains', associated with 'Iulanus son of Zeus', probably both part of a group called the

Guardians. Iulanus and Shushanna could be the real people behind the myth."

"But you said that the Guardians had an emblem of their own?"

Josiah nodded, very pleased that this attractive girl was taking such an interest in his puzzle. "The white circle on blue thing, which I think is meant to represent the full moon."

"Okay," said Nerys. "Now remind me of your other clue about the sign."

Josiah scrolled through the notes on his phone. Finding the place he read: "Nikolas, captain of ships to Iulanus Lord of Athens, hail. The coast from which the enemy fleet sailed is left empty by their ruin. There by your command we have stored and sealed your records, and the memory of Shushanna the Maid of Athens, lest some heir of Osiris should seek once more the dominion of the west. Six stadia by ship from the point, where first our sign is seen."

Nerys nodded. "So, your clue says 'our sign', not 'her sign', and if the sign of these Guardians is the full moon, that would rise in the east, and be seen first on the east coast."

"I suppose so," said Josiah, wondering if this was leading anywhere. "We hadn't thought of looking there." He got out his map of Malta and looked for the easternmost point. It wasn't easy to judge, but it appeared to be the southern tip of a bay, which stretched out just a little beyond the northern tip. Working from that point, he sketched a circle round it at approximately the right scale. It cut the coast in three places: southward, northward, and near the head of the bay. He decided it was time to have a word with his boss.

Back at the hotel, Seb was staring at maps and vaguely planning a trip to the temples on Gozo, which had never struck him as the right solution to the puzzle, but right now seemed the best he could manage. Although he trusted Josiah to take care of himself, he was relieved when his assistant reappeared, with Nerys in tow.

Josiah ran through the idea of the eastern coast search and was surprised that Seb seemed to be somewhat shaken.

"I can tell you right away about one thing that's on that very spot. It's called Bethany." Seb went on to explain why she had gone there.

"Let's get after her!" exclaimed Josiah, leaping to his feet.

"Yes!" agreed Seb. "Er, I mean no, or rather not yet. She asked me to stay away and let her use her own credentials. Let's give her the time to do that, and meet her as the dig site is closing down for the day."

Nerys asked to be involved too, and when this was agreed, first returned to her own hotel to let her family know what she would be doing.

Meanwhile Bethany had reached the abandoned hotel. Getting to Valletta had been easy, but the circular bus terminus around the Triton fountain outside the city had been confusing, and she had had to ask for help to find the Marsascala bus. However she was pleased to discover that it ran through the little town and dropped her close to her objective. The small fishing town itself did not particularly impress her. The harbour, around a kilometre long and narrow like a smaller version of those either side of Valletta, was packed with the usual colourful Maltese boats. The town was contrastingly drab, stone buildings sporting various uninspiring shades of light brown. On this dull overcast day, even the plants on the promenade managed to convey an air of tokenism rather than decoration.

Getting out her CHEOPS membership card, she walked on to the dig and introduced herself. As she anticipated, her offer to help was readily accepted, and she made herself useful at a trench that was being investigated. Later, over lunch, she was able to enquire about the discoveries which had been made already.

Local interest had been sparked by the discovery of a skeleton by men working on the former hotel. A murder investigation was soon cut short, as it became clear that the victim was ancient, though it did appear that his death had been violent. An arm bone had been badly gashed but started to heal; a deeper cut to the skull, however, had not and was presumably the immediate cause of death. Digging revealed traces of an earthwork, not very large or sophisticated. It appeared that, for reasons unknown, a group had attempted to defend the little corner of land bounded by the tip of the bay, the Mediterranean coastline, and the earthwork. No sign of a settlement had yet emerged, so possibly it was a last stand by people driven out of a village elsewhere.

Bethany fended off questions about what she was doing on Malta, still not wanting to reveal an association with Seb Lowry. In any case, she couldn't see that this dig had anything to do with the other project. To change the subject, she asked if they had tried to identify signs of the hypothetical village in the area.

The response was that it was difficult, as so much of the immediate area was built up and not accessible for archaeological work. However, the Maltese had run a speculative survey using ground penetrating radar, and had found an anomaly on the coast to the north. This had led them to a concealed tunnel, and a chamber with some astronomical decorations but nothing that indicated its origins. They had closed off the tunnel again and left any investigation to a later time. Bethany vaguely wondered about the "astronomical decorations". She decided to leave it for now but mention it to Seb later. Instead, she spent the afternoon continuing to assist at the hotel site.

As the sun began to sink, Bethany and the other workers finished their tasks and prepared to leave. She checked on where to catch the return bus, and promised to help again if her schedule – about which she was vague – permitted it. She walked off the site… and saw the person she'd asked to stay away. Annoyed, she would have ignored him, but Seb and the others were parked close to the bus stop and she had no choice but to pass them. Josiah, she observed, seemed to have acquired a girlfriend.

Of course it didn't take long to compare notes and realise that the chamber to the north, which Bethany had learned of, could easily be at one of the locations identified by Josiah and Nerys from their other clues. Seb, visibly impatient, allowed a brief stop in the centre of Marsascala for a snack, but as soon as they had finished eating he got them all back in the car and drove off up the north side of the bay.

At the mouth of the bay, the road looped round and then began to head back inland. For those wanting to stick to the coast, as they did, a well-defined dirt track veered off, as close to the shoreline as it could get on level ground. It was mostly wide enough for motor vehicles to use with room to spare, though rough enough to require caution. At a busier time it might have held the cars of a number of fishermen and bird shooters. In the fading light it was empty. They checked the map, noting that the mouth of the bay was about five hundred metres wide. That left about seven hundred metres to drive northwards.

To the left of the dirt road, endless small fields for agriculture rose up the slope, each delimited by dry stone walls. To the right, the rocky shore fell swiftly to the sea, where the east wind drove a swell against the coast. The track followed the only smooth and reasonably level ground in between.

Ahead of them, a sudden incline took the road up to a stone building, which Josiah took to be part of some island defence system. It was about the right distance from the bay and they left the car to look around.

Nerys wandered to the seaward side of the track and looked down. Suddenly she pointed. "There!" They all followed her gesture. Below them was a temporary structure which could only mark the entrance to the tunnel.

The group scrambled down the uneven slope. But Josiah hung back, grabbing his phone and chatting excitedly with his brother in London. "We may have found something big ... on the coast, just north of a town called Marsascala ... got to go now."

Seb overheard the end of the call as Josiah caught up with the others. "Who were you talking to?" he demanded angrily.

"Just my brother," came the reply.

"And who's he going to tell!" snapped Seb.

"Our friends, I ... oh, blast ... no! It's all right. I told him earlier to take his chess friend out of the loop."

Back in England, Paul Hope was already sharing the good news with the supporting prayer group by email. He didn't notice that he'd forgotten to take "George" off the address list.

Vic Osgood was relaxing, confident that the events of the previous few days had stalled Lowry's team and left him with time on his hands. When the phone rang, he answered it unhurriedly. But it was his mentor and he was in a frenzied mood, relaying the interception of Josiah's news. "Our informer got an email, they're on the coast just north of Marsascala … Get out there at once … It's on the east coast; don't you have a ******* map?!" Osgood quickly sent for his local allies and got under way.

14

Discovery

They picked their way down over rough ground to a temporary canvas structure. Chunks of rock which had been removed lay scattered around. Inside the canvas they found the beginnings of a tunnel, then an improvised padlocked door which blocked it. Seb reached in his pocket for a tool and started to pick the lock.

Bethany frowned. "You can't do it that way!" she warned, fiercely.

Seb stared, uncomprehending. "If this is where the clues are pointing, we have to get inside."

"Yes, in good time. But if this is part of an archaeological study, you mustn't just tear it apart. We have to talk to the Maltese team working across the bay, get permission, open it up with them; keep records and photographs, take it a step at a time."

Seb sneered. "Oh sure; give Mannis and his people time to arrange a cover-up. I've dealt with them before; they could be on to us at any moment." He ducked out of the shelter momentarily to glance back down the track, expecting to see signs of approaching vehicles at any moment. "Come on Josiah, let's open this thing up and see inside."

Josiah hesitated for a moment, seeing both sides of the argument. Then he nodded. "Sorry," he muttered to Bethany, "but if this is what we're looking for, we can't let the chance go." Bethany scowled.

The padlock stood no chance against Seb's experience of getting into places which he was supposed to be kept out of. Seb shone a light down the narrow passage that was revealed, and could see no further obstruction. Bethany insisted on taking a camera shot down the tunnel, before Seb pushed her away and ducked inside. One by one the group scrambled through the opening and crawled inside. Mounting excitement filled each of them as they squeezed themselves down the passageway on hands and knees. Even Bethany found the thrill of potential discoveries beginning to overwhelm her concern for following proper procedures.

It was hard to guess the tunnel's length, but it went perhaps twenty metres down and into the coastal hill, before they emerged into a precisely cut rectangular chamber. Over the millennia the tunnel had become a watercourse; they scrabbled through clinging mud and debris, and there was some standing water on the floor of the chamber. Behind them the newly risen moon, now nearing the full, beamed a shaft of light down the tunnel out of the darkening eastern sky.

"Coincidence," thought Bethany.

"Destiny?" wondered Josiah.

By both moonlight and torchlight they saw the now familiar earthly counterpart of the moonbeam, protected by some sort of glaze through the millennia; the symbol of white circle on blue, flanked by yellow stripes. Around it were various panels, in which white stones glinted as the light caught them. A flash momentarily blinded them as Bethany deployed her camera again. These panels, she realised, were the "astronomical decorations" she'd been told about.

Seb could not keep his voice from trembling. "So, the Guardians were here. But what now? Do you suppose that the panels are some sort of clue?"

Helen gave a mock shudder. "This is where the booby traps come in," she said in a high-pitched voice, feigning alarm.

"Perhaps," remarked Seb seriously. "But that possibility has been exaggerated for the sake of film audiences. I'm not too worried. The records were concealed against some future contingency. I think that the Guardians wanted them found at the right time."

"Some of the panels are constellations," Josiah noticed, confirming Bethany's thoughts. "Here's the Plough; that one's Cassiopeia; there's Orion. I don't recognise the others, but they may be star maps too."

Seb was thinking, and remembering. He turned to Bethany. "Didn't you say once that Orion was Osiris?" She nodded. "So if you were a Guardian, and Orion was your enemy, what would you want to do? Slay him, the clue said."

Seizing the Orion panel, and ignoring Bethany's protesting glare, he gave it a sharp pull and twist. It came loose, rotating to a horizontal position – the hunter lying prostrate. In response, in the right-hand wall, which had looked solid, a door creaked ajar. Now they could go beyond what the Maltese workers had already found.

"Wow!" exclaimed Josiah.

One by one, cautiously looking for any traps that might yet be lying in wait, they filed through the door. They found themselves in a large chamber which the torches struggled to light. Against the further wall, down the length of the room, stood a number of ceramic pots. But on the side walls, revealed and then disappearing as the torch beams played across them, two great maps were painted in detail. Fully five metres wide and nearly three high, they filled each wall with a mass of detail.

Seb gasped as he realised what he was seeing. On the right-hand wall the whole panorama of the globe was laid out from east to west, mapped to recognisable accuracy if not perfection. All the features he had come to expect were there: the glacier features in North America, the exaggerated river deltas, the Antarctic coastline with rivers and ice-free mountains showing, extra islands rising above the mid-Atlantic surface, rivers in the Sahara desert. It was his camera now that flashed in the darkness, getting the map on record frame by frame.

Bethany had gone immediately to take a look at the pottery. She turned round, beaming. "This is old," she said, all caution gone in a rush of excitement. "By the style, I'd say these pots are probably from the third millennium BC, the Iceman's era. I can hardly believe it, but it looks like we've done it. This is what we've been searching for."

Helen threw her arms around Seb. "Congratulations, Indiana," she cried. They hugged each other for several seconds, before Seb slowly disentangled himself and resumed his work.

Josiah was studying the other, facing wall. This map was of the portolan type, covering the Mediterranean area and points further north and east. The wind roses that framed the design were prominent. In various places drawings of people or things had overlaid the basic map. At the western end, nearest the entrance, a giant human figure rose from the Iberian peninsula almost to the ceiling, where above him shone an array of stars. Further east was the leg of Italy, and above it the Alps. Somewhere on the southern slopes of the Alps a town in flames was depicted. Josiah's gaze continued eastward. On the Greek mainland, somewhere near present day Athens, three characters were grouped: a man and woman arrayed for battle, and another giant, this one clad in skins and carrying a club. Josiah recognised the traditional depiction of the hero Heracles – or Hercules in the Latin. Above the trio, near the top of the wall, hung a painting of a strangely unblemished full moon, no seas and few craters marked in it. Further east still, two more tall figures stood on the Nile delta and the region of Israel, the latter in priestly-looking robes. And on the extreme right of the map, beyond the normal portolan range, another huge figure stood beside a steeply rising tower on the Euphrates river. Like the man on the extreme left, he was crowned with stars, this time in the immediately recognisable Orion shape. Next to him, dwarfed but still big enough to convey significance, was another man, in robes bearing a rainbow motif. Between all these major figures were a host of smaller pictures, harder to make out. In places the protective glaze was long gone and the paint had flaked away. The impression was of fleets and armies on the move, marching out in all directions from the great tower, while others converged on Greece from west and east.

Below the map, reaching down to the floor so that they had to stoop to see them clearly, were a number of close-up scenes outside the main picture. Below the Nile delta, the skin-clad giant appeared again, pointing to the west with an urgent gesture. Underneath Greece, a branch was shown, bearing slender leaves and a small, dark fruit. Seb recalled the ancient tale that the first Athenians had chosen Athena because she offered them the olive tree. Moving left, below the central Mediterranean appeared a ship with the moon and stripes banner flying, then next to that was shown a bearded figure, with a baby in his arms and his right hand resting in blessing on a small boy. In the leftmost picture, a dark-haired swimming figure raised a knife to slice through the anchor line of a ship. Something made Josiah grin as he noted which of the other figures on the full map was depicted with particularly dark hair.

Seb switched his focus to the portolan map. For all his elation, something was troubling him. The others could not guess what. "What have we here?" he asked, half talking to himself, but loud enough to be heard.

"I'd say it looks like our key players," said Josiah. "The guy on the left should be Atlas; he's tall enough to be holding up the sky. The trio in Greece are Heracles for certain, and maybe Zeus and Athena from the rhyme, though they don't look like the usual representations. In fact they do look a bit Neanderthal, whatever Bethany would say about that."

"What about the pair from our Cornish inscription – Iulanus and Shushanna?" asked Seb.

"Could be," nodded Josiah.

Another thought occurred to Seb. "Or it could be both – the same people under two different names."

Josiah nodded again, and added, "On the right we have Nimrod at the Tower of Babel."

"But depicted as Orion/Osiris," broke in Bethany. "Now, the rainbow symbol should denote Noah, but Noah should be a figure of at least Nimrod's stature. I'd guess we're looking at a descendant or successor. Interesting too that there's a priestly figure near Jerusalem. This is far too old for it to be a Jewish priest. Babel was long before the Exodus, long before Abraham even."

"There was a priest-king at Jerusalem in Abraham's time," said Josiah. "Melchizedek, or some such name. Maybe the tradition of it being a holy city goes back before the time of the Jews."

Seb stared at the painting, and ran his torch over each part again and again. For someone in his hour of triumph, he seemed strangely subdued. They waited for him to gather his thoughts, until Helen could bear the suspense no longer. "This is the sort of find you've always dreamed of. What is the matter with you?"

Seb shook his head. "It just doesn't add up. The glacier maps and the ice-free Antarctic, they don't belong together. They have to be two different periods – Ice Age and a warm spell. And Babel, and Nimrod – they should be at the dawn of conventionally known history, say around three thousand BC, whereas Atlas belongs about nine or ten thousand BC. It's like all the bits and pieces from different times have been jumbled together. I don't understand it at all."

"Then just record it for now," said Bethany. "We can do the theories later, but getting the data on film has to be done now."

Seb roused himself from his perplexity and started filming again. "But if this is a jumble of different times, it's a later depiction – not original at all. It doesn't get us further forward." The dream find still looked jaded.

Bethany tried to reassure him. "As I said before, the pottery is ancient. And the place doesn't look to have been disturbed. I think it's significant. We just have some figuring out to do later."

They resumed the process of documenting and photographing the room. Bethany, with Nerys, discovered some old parchments in another of the pots. She marvelled at the preservation – this was something that had been made to last, possibly using some lost technique. The language looked Greek; she would have to get help to translate it. The white circle on blue appeared again, apparently marking sections in the documents.

Josiah was examining the fine detail of the portolan. "There are various spots marked with small banners," he said. "It reminds me of a war zone map – different flags for the different sides. Southwest Britain has a moon banner, which should mark it as Guardian territory. There are star banners in France, Spain, Italy – north and south, Malta, central North Africa... I guess that marks the other side. Moving further east: moon banners on Crete, Greece, Israel – some way north of Jerusalem, and the Nile delta..." His voice tailed off as he heard a noise from outside the room.

They all stopped to listen. Someone else was crawling down the tunnel. "I bet that's Mannis's people," said Seb softly. "They probably followed us here somehow. Can we shut the door and keep them out?" He pushed it to, but it swung loosely back. He swore.

"It's just as well," commented Bethany dryly. "There's no handle on this side; you would have shut us in! Does it matter if they find us? It makes no difference to what we've discovered."

Seb pondered. "The trouble is, they've already stooped to staging thefts and trying to bribe you, to keep us off a pretty cryptic trail. If something is being covered up, what will they do to keep a find as clear as this a secret?"

Helen paled, but then an idea struck her. "Isn't there another way out?" They all stared at her. "Well, there would be in a film – a shaft, an air vent, or... something..." She trailed off, inspiration failing. But Bethany kept the ball rolling.

"Air vent? I'd say yes, the builders would have needed ventilation." Her torch swept across the ceiling, then down the wall beside the door by which they had entered. Something glinted. Here were more of the star panels, like the one that had opened the door. Above them was the symbol of the Guardians, just like in the first room. She moved towards them. As she approached, she felt a breeze on her hair. She looked up, but saw no gap in the ceiling. "There's a down draught. We need to try to go up the vent. Up. What sign might denote up? There's a star sign that's a leaping goat, isn't there?"

"Capricorn," said Josiah. "I'm afraid I wouldn't recognise that."

"What else? Up! Hermes? Hermes was a winged messenger, wasn't he?"

"Yes," said Josiah, "but Hermes would be Mercury, and that's a planet, not a star sign. There was a winged horse though – er... Pegasus." He searched for a memory. "Near Andromeda... the Square of Pegasus."

Bethany spotted a block with a square of stars and gave it a twist, then, finding no movement, a pull. It came out of the wall, waist high, several inches towards her. There was a noise of rumbling movement and the draught suddenly strengthened. Beside her head a panel in the world map wall opened up. Bethany pulled herself up and then through the hole. Her torch showed her a tunnel. "This is the back door. Quick." She reached down and helped as, one after the other, Helen, Nerys, Josiah and Seb followed into the vent.

As Seb hung from the opening, he gave the Pegasus block a kick back into position. It retracted smoothly into the wall. Bethany and Josiah hurriedly pulled him up as the vent closed in response. Now it was just a crack again. Helen and Nerys were already prospecting the tunnel beyond. Helen turned to urge the others on, but Seb flashed his torch to show a finger to his lips. They froze, waiting.

Into the chamber strode Vic Osgood, a gun in his hand and a similarly armed escorting quartet behind him. At the sight of an empty room and dead end he paused. He knew Lowry's party had entered the underground complex; where could they have gone? "Is there some other way out of here?"

"More star panels behind here," reported one of his companions.

Osgood looked, trying to think clearly. Adrenalin and anxiety were clouding his mind. "They must have guessed somehow how to open the first door. Trial and error, perhaps. Which panel controls the way out?" He scanned the wall, but everything was now back in place. "Pegasus, Andromeda, Gemini, Pisces, Cancer." He knew his constellations, at any rate. "A horse, a princess, twins, fishes, crab. What do they mean?" He glared at the symbol above them. "Curse the Man of Division!" he exclaimed, and smashed a fist on the moon symbol. Immediately the floor opened beneath his feet. He fell, and his closest companion pitched forward too, landing on top of him a good ten feet down. More curses filled the chamber. "Lowry? How do you get out of this? Lowry! If you know, help us!"

"Not likely." The voice echoed around. Osgood couldn't tell where it was coming from. It didn't matter anyway. Seb Lowry and his party were scrambling out the exit tunnel.

The last foot presented some difficulty. The passage narrowed to a small hole, virtually undetectable from outside. Helen, in the lead, was temporarily baffled, but Seb squeezed past her and quickly clawed the earth away with his hands. They found themselves only a matter of yards from the tunnel by which they had entered. They were able to scramble down to level ground, and started to pick their way back to the car. It was now dark apart from the moonlight.

Suddenly barking broke out near them, and a torch flashed. Stumbling across the rocks, they saw Osgood and his men emerging. Osgood stooped to two dogs that had been tethered by the canvas shelter. "You were bred by Orion for the hunt. Now find his enemies!"

Seb's party scrambled into their car as the dogs came at them. It was a tight squeeze on the back seat. Seb swung the car round and sent it forward as fast as he dared on the rough terrain. They passed two cars parked nearby – the ones in which Osgood's party had arrived. In his haste to chase Lowry down, Osgood had neglected to position his vehicles so as to obstruct an escape.

A shot cracked out and they all ducked. "Are they shooting at us?" Helen's voice was as high as fear could drive it.

"Just trying to disable the car," muttered Seb as he risked more throttle and the car bucked on stones.

"Are you sure?" squeaked Helen.

From low behind Seb's seat came some muffled words in Bethany's tones. They caught the terms "unscientific" and "speculation".

Osgood and his men leapt into the other cars and turned them in pursuit. Seb drove on grimly, while his three young charges bumped about in the back and Helen tried to find her seatbelt. Where the dirt track met the road there was room for only one car, and a hapless local was about to enter. Seb hit horn and accelerator simultaneously. The local stopped short and watched one, then two, then three cars speed past him.

As they swung past a small stadium, Seb took the bend on the wrong side of the road, trusting to luck that nothing was coming the other way. There was just enough room between parked cars for a bit of weaving to find the fastest line. On their left, the waters of the bay lurked as the penalty for a misjudgement. Nerys glanced across it and rued deciding to come on this trip. Seb wanted to turn away from the bay and dodge down side streets, but he needed to gain a bit of ground first. He pressed on the accelerator again.

"Humped zebra cross..." recalled Josiah from their earlier passage, his words ending in a collective scream as they hit it and bounced about again.

"Humps belong on camels, not zebras," growled Seb.

Ahead was a fork and Helen could tell he was shaping for a right turn. "No entry!" she screamed just in time. Seb swerved the car violently and just made the left fork.

Osgood barrelled past the sign anyway, hoping for a shortcut. He hit the wheel in frustration as the road turned into a cul-de-sac. Quickly he reversed and took a side route back to the bayside. The other chasing car now led him.

The road widened as it passed the distinctive church of St Anne. Beyond it a road led uphill. Seb looked at it hopefully, but saw another car coming down. Again pumping horn and accelerator – he was getting quite coordinated at combining the two – Seb charged in front of it and continued along the bay. Momentarily the pursuers were baulked, but as their horns rang out in unison the other driver let them through. His shout of anger was lost in the roaring of engines. They were now heading for the centre of town at the head of the bay.

Seb braked a little for a left turn, which he barely made as the road started to swing round towards the southern side of the bay. He wanted to turn right for Valletta, but saw a red light and an approaching line of traffic just in time. The adrenalin of the chase was sharpening his reflexes. So it was a left fork again, past a 'give way' sign, and out ahead of the traffic from the direction of Valletta. More horn blowing signified disapproval of his pace and recklessness.

The pursuers were less fortunate. Trying to follow Seb on to the main road, the lead driver pranged a car as he tried to slot into the traffic. Both came to a stop, and the occupants started a furious row. Behind them, Osgood was forced to stand on his brakes. He squealed to a stop, unhurt but unable to find a way through to continue the chase.

Seb charged uphill. But realising they were clear of pursuers, his mood calmed and he started to slow down. He gestured at their map of Malta. "Someone tell me how to find Sliema without back-tracking."

"What was Osgood going on about?" asked Bethany, as they began to relax. "Who is the Man of Division? It's not you, is it?" she added with a grin.

"I've no idea," smiled Seb. "But I see a pattern. Slay Orion/Nimrod and you make progress. Declare yourself an enemy by smiting the moon symbol thing – I had just enough view to see Osgood hit it – you get your comeuppance."

15

Review

N ext morning, the group reconvened in Seb and Helen's room after breakfast. Their rented car was parked well away from the hotel, to avoid giving away their location. So far there was no sign that Osgood had picked up their trail.

Josiah kept fiddling with his phone. He'd used it the previous evening for a few pictures, though the lighting had been poor, but he had found himself unable to send them out. At first he had thought it was because there was no signal underground, but after resurfacing and then still this morning he was having no success. Something seemed to be blocking the signal. Bethany, meanwhile, was getting Seb's photos of the maps loaded on to her tablet.

They had hardly slept for excitement and had thought a lot about the find, but were no nearer a conclusion. Josiah was puzzled by the presumed territorial markers that he'd spotted. "I thought we had a link between Cornwall and the Tyrol, but the map shows them as being on opposite sides. And here in Malta, the chamber itself seems to belong to the Guardians, but the banner on the map says it is not."

Seb tried to review the evidence in his mind. "There was evidence of a massacre in Italy, remember. If we are dealing with relics from the time of Atlantis, then we would expect to see a movement eastwards as Atlantis tried to dominate the Mediterranean. Maybe they took Italy from the Guardians by force.

And Malta, I've thought for some time, is the obvious jumping off point for an attack on Athens from the west, which is the scenario in Plato's account. Think of the massive harbours around Valletta, how big a fleet could be assembled there."

"So what are traces of the Guardians doing on Malta?" asked Josiah. "Was that captured as well?"

Seb pondered. "Maybe. Though what we are seeing is a record of the history, not the story itself. Atlantis was destroyed, remember. If the chamber was set up after that event, Malta would no longer have been Atlantean territory. What was the quotation on the Piali map?" He checked his papers. "'The coast from which the enemy fleet sailed is left empty by their ruin. There by your command we have stored and sealed your records, lest some heir of Osiris should seek once more the dominion of the west.' After the cataclysm, the danger was from Nimrod/Osiris, which means Mesopotamia or Egypt. West of Athens would have been safer than eastwards."

"What I don't understand," put in Helen, "is, why set up a store here at all? Wouldn't it have been easier to keep the records in Athens itself?"

Seb had to agree, but suggested that the Malta chamber could be a sort of backup version. "Maybe Athens was vulnerable. It seems that they still feared the heirs of Nimrod. Probably there are additional records to be found in Greece, if we knew where to look."

Seb felt reasonably satisfied with that as a provisional explanation. But again and again he returned to the chronological problem. "We have the last Ice Age and the Atlas/Atlantis stuff, which is around nine or ten thousand BC. And we have the Tower of Babel, Nimrod/Osiris and the Guardians, which we know are third millennium BC. And we have them together. There has to be around a seven thousand year gap between them. It just doesn't add up."

Bethany agreed with Seb's definition of the problem. "Get the chronology right and everything else can fall into place. That's always been the thinking behind the New Chronology for Egypt, and it will work here as well. We just have to keep trying alternatives, until we finds one that fits."

"What we do have here is evidence of two source maps, from which the ones in the chamber and the other extant copies were drawn. One is the standard portolan covering the Mediterranean, the other is the world map like the Piri Re'is and Piali maps; two different traditions utilising the same skills."

This insight brightened Seb's mood a little. He added his own comment, that there could be more traditions of map-making involved. "The Guardians seem to have been penned into the Eastern Mediterranean. They had the skills to draw the maps, as we've seen; but not the opportunity to gather all the data. The surveying of South America, Antarctica and so forth must have been done by the other side, the Atlanteans and Osiris."

Nerys tossed out an idea that was bothering her. "The pictures along the bottom of the Mediterranean map – any ideas what they mean?"

"Only one," replied Seb. "The olive branch below Athens. I think that ties in with the ancient story that Poseidon and Athena offered the Athenians a gift in return for their worship. Athena offered the olive tree and that was the one they accepted. And if I remember rightly, Poseidon is said to be the father of Atlas, so" – thinking it through as he said it – "maybe that was what set in motion Plato's conflict between Atlantis and Athens."

"So are you saying those little pictures are underneath the places that they relate to?" queried Josiah.

Seb considered briefly. "Could be. But what of it?"

"Well, the picture of the man blessing the boy would be under the Tyrol, wouldn't it? Which is the area that we think may have changed hands. Just a thought, but maybe that scene goes back to when the Tyrol was Guardian territory, and the boy being blessed was the one who would grow up to be the Guardians' leader."

"Iulanus," mused Seb, stroking his chin as he thought. "And the baby became the woman shown with him in Greece. Yes, that could fit. I don't know how we prove it, but it's possible. And then the swimmer cutting the ship's anchor refers to something which took place in the western Med."

"Er, no," put in Josiah with a grin. "That picture is also underneath Cornwall. And there were only two figures in the whole thing shown with jet black hair – the swimmer, and the Athena/Shushanna figure in Greece. I think they're the same person. A woman wrecking a ship. Allowing for the tale becoming garbled over time... Bethany, we've found your mermaid!"

Bethany glared at him, then countered with excessive sarcasm. "I hope she comes with a wetsuit. Swimming in Ice Age waters wouldn't be healthy."

Josiah was suddenly lost in thought. "I need to look something up," he muttered, and turned for the door. Nerys followed him out of the room.

Bethany and Seb's discussion roamed on and on, never finding a satisfactory solution. Helen hung around, spending most of the time gazing out of the window and only half listening. She wasn't prepared to leave Seb and Bethany alone in a bedroom, even if it was doubling as their work centre.

Seb kept running over various possibilities. "Maybe the stuff we found yesterday was painted, say, three thousand years ago. Then the two memories – of the Atlantis/Ice Age era and the Babel era – might have already been confused. We need to keep looking; there has to be something further back that will show one tradition but not the other."

"That's OK to explain the maps," said Bethany, "but the pottery was pretty archaic by the standards of three thousand years ago. I checked my books and it definitely points to the Babel era, the third millennium BC. We can't just dismiss that."

"It's the Antarctic depiction that really gets me," confessed Seb. "That can't possibly be Ice Age; it has to mean there was a period of global warming more recently. Unless that bit is just a coincidence... But it's shown with the glacier indications in the northern hemisphere. How can that make sense?"

Helen had an idea. "What about the effect of ocean currents?"

Seb and Bethany swung round sharply. They had been so absorbed in their discussion that they had almost forgotten Helen's presence. "What do you mean?" asked Seb.

"You remember when you were looking round the pyramids and temples in Peru," said Helen, "and I went off to the coast and found all those penguins? They survive in the tropics because they get the benefit of a cold water current from the Southern Ocean; and in Cornwall, all those gardens with warm weather plants, because of the Gulf Stream. Maybe the Antarctic was once warmed by a current like the Gulf Stream."

The other two were happy to acknowledge that this was at least a possibility. But even if true, they could see no way to prove it. And where would such a current come from, and how powerful would it have to be? "I know where most of today's main ocean currents are," said Seb, "because that relates to what voyages were possible, using them in ancient times. I thought that the Antarctic is surrounded by a circular cold current, very large and very powerful, driven by the winds of the Roaring Forties. I'd like to believe in your warm water current, dear, but I don't see how it could be strong enough."

By noon, Bethany was ready for an early lunch. Her enthusiasm had gradually evaporated as the evidence failed to fit each and every attempt to interpret it. But outside her room, Nerys was waiting. "Come down to the Internet room," she said. "Josiah remembered a very interesting possibility; he's been looking into it online. Fortunately this place still has a hardwired online connection, because we still can't get a wireless one. We want to show you what we're looking at before trying it on Seb."

Mystified, and pausing only for a biscuit and quick mouthful of fruit juice, Bethany followed her downstairs. They found Josiah intent on a computer screen. Apart from a couple of Net surfers, who were unlikely to bother with a lunch break, they had the room to themselves.

Bethany looked at the screen. Then she recoiled with surprise and a certain amount of indignation. "The Ice Age and Noah's flood," she recited. "What is this?"

"Believe it or not, it's hard science," said Josiah. "The basic theory came out years ago; this is a new refinement of the analysis. I've seen plenty of maths to back it up, though I don't follow that too well myself and you might not either. No evolutionist has ever come up with a good explanation for Ice Ages. But if you start with Noah's Flood and plug those initial conditions into a climate model, you get a very convincing solution."

Bethany interrupted. She wasn't going to have pseudoscience thrust on to her research project. "Hold it there. We know what causes Ice Ages; it's natural variations in the Earth's orbit over tens of thousands of years. The theory is well established."

"But doesn't explain the full magnitude of the climate changes," continued Josiah smoothly. "It stands up to some extent, but only because no one who believes in a millions of years history can come up with anything better. Its supporters have to invoke unknown feedback mechanisms, which are assumed to magnify the effects of the orbital changes. There's no need for Bible-believing Christians like us to stick to long age restrictions."

Bethany glared. Her sarcasm was working overtime. "And the Flood is the answer? What, like all the water froze when Noah came out of the Ark, perhaps?"

Josiah grinned. "Certainly not. Just suppose for one moment that the Flood was real, okay? You can change your mind again later."

Bethany didn't mind putting up a hypothesis to be knocked straight back down; it was one way to disprove it. "Go on," she said grimly.

"Well, the water was not freezing. Far from it; most of it had come from the depths of the earth, the "fountains of the great deep", as the Bible calls it. That means it would be warm – hot even. Probably so warm that Noah almost needed to have fish on the Ark to stop them frying. That's why, when you said about the Ice Age seas being too cold for a mermaid, I felt something wasn't right and it reminded me of all this stuff."

Bethany realised the remark about the fish wasn't serious, but laughed in spite of herself at the thought of fish having to escape from the Flood in a tank on the ark.

"Warm water means lots of evaporation," the explanation continued, "and then lots of rain, or, in colder regions, lots of snow.

As the land cooled because of dust in the air from volcanic eruptions, but the oceans for a time remained warm, snow fell in much larger quantities than today. Once it started falling quicker in winter than it could melt in summer, an Ice Age followed. Eventually the oceans cooled to today's temperature, and the eruptions stopped as the planet got back to normal, so evaporation fell to today's levels, and the melting took over. End of Ice Age – start of modern climates. The transition is reckoned to have taken several centuries. The original model estimated seven hundred years, give or take a bit. This new paper refines the estimate slightly.

"And while this was going on," Josiah added, "you would have glaciers inland and warm climate on the coasts, giving you Ice Age conditions in Scandinavia and North America, but a more moderate climate than today at the edge of Antarctica, maybe enough to make it accessible."

"We were speculating upstairs about a source of warm water as a factor," said Bethany, remembering Helen's suggestion. But she wasn't ready to admit that this scenario could be valid. "And just when did all this happen?" she asked, still maintaining an icy tone.

Josiah took up the tale again. "If you take everything literally, the Bible puts the flood at around 2350 BC. Some people argue that there are gaps in the genealogies, which would make the flood a little earlier. Others say you can't compromise on the genealogies without undermining the whole Bible. Frankly I find that debate a little tiresome. We should be establishing that the Flood really happened, to convince the unbelievers, not arguing among ourselves about when."

"But knowing when would help to establish if it could be real," pointed out Bethany. "Or not." The sarcasm was waxing again. "I suppose the people who date a worldwide Flood at 2350 BC suppose that somehow the Egyptian civilization just carried on through it. Or do they dismiss the archaeology?"

Josiah paused to think. Nerys answered for him. "That could be a weak point," she conceded. "I got hold of a book which tried to tie the archaeological record of history to the biblical dates, but I didn't think much of it. The whole area is still a work in progress.

I'd simply say that Noah's flood occurred just like the Bible tells it, but I don't know when exactly. I guess it would have to be before your Egyptian kingdoms – pick a date that suits you."

"How about 3113 BC?" broke in Josiah. "That's when the Maya calendar for this era of world history starts. That should leave a bit of space for population to recover, and for the Egyptian kingdoms we know about to get started."

Bethany turned her gaze to the computer screen. She motioned for the mouse, which Josiah relinquished, and started scrolling. There were pages of argument and equations. It certainly looked like a real scientific paper.

Josiah was expounding again. "Of course, Egypt in the Ice Age would have been a lot wetter than today, less dependent on the Nile, because there was more rain generally. The need to depend on the Nile floods would have gradually increased. I don't know if the archaeology supports that."

Bethany frowned. "Actually, it does. People have argued that the climate became significantly drier during the Old Kingdom. That's certainly the CHEOPS view."

"After the Sphinx got its rain weathering," suggested Josiah. Bethany turned a glare on him. He shrugged. "Sorry, I mean got eroded by natural drainage. The pyramids would have to date from after the wet period though. Hey, looks like the Sphinx could go back to the Ice Age after all, without needing to be ten thousand years old to do so."

"Which would put the Flood date back further," mused Bethany. "Only by a couple of hundred years though; the pyramids went up around twenty four hundred or twenty five hundred BC. In any case, the outermost layer of the Giza pyramids has largely disappeared. Maybe that casing layer did get eroded, before the stones were reused." The others waited for a new attempt at a refutation. Bethany couldn't immediately think of one. This ball was running rather further than she'd expected.

"Sea level rose at the end of the Ice Age," continued Josiah. "That could have left the layer at Ur which was once thought to be from Noah's flood, maybe around three thousand BC or a bit later. And could have drowned Atlantis."

Bethany stared at him. "You're putting Atlantis at around two or three thousand BC? Have you told Plato?"

"Yes," said Josiah, "I was looking through Seb's copy of Plato's account earlier. Plato does repeatedly say Atlantis was nine thousand years ago, but at one point he specifies that Atlantis was a thousand years before the start of Egyptian civilization, which he puts at eight thousand years before his time. But suppose that date for Egypt is off the mark."

"The Egyptians had an exaggerated idea of their own history, for sure," agreed Bethany. "And if Plato didn't, or couldn't, check his sources..."

"...he just reproduced their error," finished Josiah.

"So," Bethany was trying to gather the lines of thought, "Mesopotamia gets disrupted at the end of the Ice Age, by the flooding of Ur, if nothing else. Atlantis gets drowned at the end of the Ice Age, and Egyptian culture rises from the ruins. All at around the same time. You say this" – she gestured at the screen – "is all legitimate science?" Nerys and Josiah both nodded. "And you compress the timeline so much, you could probably have Neanderthal traits persisting as recently as Babel?" she mused, ending it as a question.

"Certainly," said Josiah. "One creationist theory to explain typical Neanderthal traits is that they are a natural consequence of living for hundreds of years; they died out as the average lifetime decreased after the Flood."

"I thought that there were known child fossils with Neanderthal traits," muttered Bethany. "I'll look that up later. Oh well, first you want to make me find Atlantis, now you want to make me a creationist. God, is there any chance of me having a sensible career some day?" Bethany's glare would have turned skywards if she had dared.

She paused. Deep inside a voice seemed to whisper, "You haven't *got* to find Atlantis." The thought made her wonder. The linking up with Lowry, the turning down of what seemed to be a better offer, had it all been a stage to go through to lead her to this? Was there really something in this creationist business, which everything she knew about science told her was an anachronism?

"There's something else that this scenario explains," put in Josiah.

"And what's that?" asked Bethany sharply, wondering what aspect of her thinking was going to be challenged next.

"Why they bothered mapping, and maybe settling, Antarctica at all," said Josiah, "if it was done just after the poles had shifted (which everyone who's considered the problem, except Seb, has argued). They should have known that an ice cap would re-form at the new pole, and the land would become valueless and inaccessible. But if the mapmakers were the early post-Flood generations, they would not have expected that. The pre-Flood world is thought to have been warm, with no polar ice; the immediate post-Flood oceans were warm; they would not have foreseen the big freeze around the poles."

At that moment Helen came bursting into the room. "Oh, there you are. Time to pack!" she announced.

"Has Osgood found us?" asked Josiah in panic.

"No. He's pulled some strings, and doesn't need to find us himself. The island bureaucracy have done the job for him. We are not wanted on Malta; we are to hand over all our records, pack our gear, proceed directly to the airport and take the next flight home."

"That's what comes of living in a super-state," muttered Josiah. More loudly he added, "Who is 'we'?"

"Sebastian Lowry, Helen Carr, Bethany Fisher and Josiah Hope," declaimed Helen. "Persona non grata on Malta. No appeal. So go pack. I don't like it either, but we have no choice."

Bethany and Josiah reluctantly got up.

"One moment," said Nerys. Josiah eagerly turned back towards her. "How do they know what 'all your records' are? Leave some with me. Just hand over enough to look convincing."

"Are you sure?" queried Josiah.

"Sure," confirmed Nerys. "They're clearly not on to me. And who is going to stop the family of a customs officer? It does mean you'll have to get in touch with me back in England. I suppose," she pretended reluctance but was smiling, "I'll have to give you my phone number."

"Yes, I suppose so," said Josiah, also pretending reluctance. "Well, Seb must have a lot to worry about, so I'll take care of that small detail for him."

"Good idea," said Nerys, still smiling. "I'll come and help you sort through stuff, what to give up and what I can keep for you."

"It's worth a try," said Bethany, "if you're prepared to take the chance."

"I am," said Nerys.

16

Back Home

Seb sat in his study, dumbfounded. His team were back home and reviewing their discoveries over cups of hot tea or coffee. "You tell me that the answers are in the Bible? I mean, I've known all along that you're both Christians, but surely you believe in science too? The six days of creation were disproved in the nineteenth century."

Bethany frowned. "I don't like it either. I thought I knew how to reconcile my science and my faith. But I've twisted the data this way and that in my mind, and nothing else seems to fit. Show me another solution." She could almost have added, "Please!"

Seb shook his head. "I wish I had one. Maybe I just need more time to think. But surely you can't just say God created everything, and ignore all the evidence for evolution."

Josiah looked straight at him, the things which he'd seen falling into place in their investigation making him confident. Several times he'd ducked confrontation, but now he decided to accept the challenge. "What evidence for evolution?" he asked.

Seb stared back, more nonplussed than ever. "I beg your pardon?"

"What evidence for evolution?" repeated Josiah. "Show me your evidence."

Seb blinked in bafflement. Then he swung round and pulled a file from the bookshelf behind him. He had cuttings from many different scientific magazines, all neatly sorted and labelled. This one read "Evolution".

"Here you are. 'The evidence for evolution is overwhelming.' And here: 'No serious scientists have any sympathy with the fundamentalist rednecks who deny the fact of evolution.' Shall I go on?"

"But don't you see?" said Josiah. "All they're saying is that everyone believes it, so it must be true. They don't show you the evidence. Go through any number of articles, you'll find the same thing. And do you know why?" When Seb offered no answer, he continued. "It's because they know that if they cite anything specific, the refutation will appear on creationist websites in a few days, if it's not already there. The evolutionists have no evidence. Their claims melt away when examined."

Seb racked his brains for memories of science lessons. "What about the peppered moths?" he said at length.

"What about them?" replied Josiah.

"What do they teach you at school?" sighed Seb. "The moths turned darker when there was a lot of pollution in the atmosphere, and lighter again when the pollution was cleaned up. They evolved camouflage to fit their surroundings. I thought everyone knew that."

Josiah grinned. "They were still moths, weren't they?"

Seb glared. "Of course they were still moths. What else would they be?"

"But don't you see? Evolution claims that moths can turn into other creatures, that dinosaurs could turn into birds, apes turned into men, and so on. Don't show me variations within a kind of animal, variations based on the genetic capacity that God built into them, and try to tell me that it means that one kind can turn into another. Take Darwin's finches as another example. They're still finches. Go back to the Galapagos in a million years' time and they'll still be finches." Josiah was looking confident.

Bethany had grasped the point, but this kind of argument was still new to her. Part of her still hoped to find a flaw. She decided to test it further. "What about super bugs – the germs that evolve resistance to antibiotics? I realise they're still germs, but doesn't it show how they can mutate further given enough time?"

Josiah tried to remember. "Super bugs... super bugs. I might have to look up some references on that. No, I remember now, I read about them a few months ago. Do you know how they evolve resistance?" Bethany shook her head, as did Seb. "They lose the component which the antibiotics attack. Outside the hospital environment, they are less fit than the other bugs, so they die out. You might call it evolution, but it's backwards – a loss of genetic information rather than a gain."

"Backwards evolution," mused Bethany. "Like the life spans in Genesis getting shorter and shorter over time?"

"Exactly," said Josiah.

"I give up," said Seb, frowning. "I mean, thanks for your time and effort and all that, but if you're going to stick by creationism, I don't see how we can continue to work together. I'll pay you in full for the work you've put in, but I think our association is over."

The other two slowly digested this. Josiah looked down at his feet. "It's your call," he said at length. "I would love to see you believe, but I can't make you. Thanks for giving me the opportunity to work with you and to share in your research."

Seb switched his gaze. "And you, Bethany?"

"I'm still making my mind up," she said frankly. "I'll call you if I think of another answer that fits what we've found. I mean that," she added, seeing Seb look doubtful. "And like Josiah said, thanks and all that. I'm sort of learning that God will lead me through messy situations, not leave me stuck in them. One day I'll see what the next step is."

The meeting broke up.

Professor Mannis was satisfied and happy for once. He beamed as he welcomed Vic Osgood and Doctor Laude into his study. "I've just had word from Malta. The chambers you found have been cleared out and washed clean. So Lowry's had all his expedition records confiscated, and if he tells anyone what he saw, there's no longer any evidence to back him up. He either keeps quiet or makes himself look a fool. He's usually better at the latter, but this time I think even he will see sense."

Osgood was relieved. "And do we have any word from Hope's brother?"

"Yes, and that's good as well. They can't reconcile the two time zones on the map they claim to have seen. Part of it looks to be ten thousand years old or more, while other parts look to be from around three thousand BC. That's always been the problem for everyone who's looked into the ancient maps issue. They're no further forward than when they started."

"But what was it they found?" Osgood wanted to know.

"Well," said Doctor Laude, "if they only knew, I'd say that they found exactly what they were looking for. The white circle device that you foolishly hit is, according to our information, the emblem of the followers of the Man of Division, in Europe at least. And the Mediterranean map showed the whole pattern of resistance to Osiris, a defensive alliance centred on Athens and coming under increasing pressure from Osiris to the east and his allies to the west. So, the Treasures of Zeus are no more. One more threat to the restoration of Osiris's dream of world unity has been dealt with."

"We're having a celebration in London on Friday evening," said Mannis. "The usual venue. I expect to see both of you there."

Bethany had gone round to see Josiah and Paul. It was a few weeks after their return from Malta, and Christmas decorations now brightened the Hopes' front room. "Seb won't accept it, and he says he's got no evidence left to present in a book, but the more I think about it, the more I find myself concluding that we're on the right track. It's a real stunner. Almost as big a switch in view as becoming a Christian in the first place. Bigger, in some ways, because when I asked Jesus into my heart I had only a vague idea of what was happening, I learnt more as I went along. This has hit me all at once."

"So you're a creationist now," Josiah sounded pleased.

Bethany still wanted to hedge. "There are a lot of things in the creationist case that I'm not sure of. I'd need to be an expert in a dozen fields to evaluate all the stuff I've been reading. What I am prepared to say is that on this issue it looks as if the creationist model is the one that fits the evidence. There is one thing which bothers me though – I've been looking at the typical creationist timeline and there's no room for our mapmakers between the Flood and Babel. Only just over a century, though that isn't based completely on the Bible. There just wouldn't be enough people around by then for all the scenes on that map in the Maltese chamber."

Josiah nodded, looking thoughtful. "I've been wondering about that too. The best I can come up with is that the Genesis account is only an outline, and there was more going on than it tells us. But I know it would be very hard to sell that line to the typical creationist. I hope we find out some day. But first, I've got another shock for you." Bethany looked worried. Josiah explained. "It occurred to me last night. We didn't need to do all this work."

"What?" exclaimed Bethany.

"The ancient maps were known," explained Josiah. "The creation science Ice Age model has been around for years. All we did was see stuff which backs it up. The business about the Guardians, Zeus and Athena, or Iulanus and Shushanna, or whoever, is all very interesting. But it's incidental. The theory we think we've confirmed can be put forward from what was already known."

Bethany tried to digest this. "But having extra information is bound to help in the long run. It will come in useful some time."

"What we do know," pointed out Paul, "is that someone is very interested in keeping all this quiet. I've been careful to tell our supposed 'prayer supporter' George that we are completely baffled by what you saw. I think he's happy about that."

"Yes," said Josiah. "I hope we get to the bottom of that eventually. Meanwhile, I think I've worked something else out. You remember what Osgood said before he fell through the floor of the hidden chamber?"

"'Curse the Man of Division', wasn't it?" said Bethany. "Whatever that means."

"Try Genesis 10 verse 25," said Josiah with a smile. "'Two sons were born to Eber: one was named Peleg, because in his time the earth was divided…' Peleg was the patriarch alive at the time of the Tower of Babel. He comes halfway between Noah and Abraham, on the direct line of descent. I bet he was the guy shown wearing the rainbow robes; dwarfed by Nimrod in worldly stature, but still a significant opponent. So the Man of Division was a good guy. Quite a surprise to our way of thinking, which values unity so highly."

"Unity is only good if you're united on the right side," said Paul.

"Nimrod's unity was the wrong sort," added Josiah. "God had to step in and judge it before it did irreparable harm. And what particularly interests me, though it will be too political for your liking, is that some people have traced the modern moves towards a world super-state back to Nimrod. There's supposedly a direct chain, although the links are well hidden and very hard to prove, through secret Egyptian priestly knowledge, on to modern Freemasonry and other secret societies. I think that God has shown us this so that we can act on it somehow – warn people what's going on behind the scenes."

"What sort of case can you present?" asked Bethany. "Assuming you're right, that is. I'm not convinced yet. Though if I'm to end up as a creationist Atlantis hunter instead of a respectable scientist, I suppose I might just as well be a political crank as well. Go the whole hog. We lost all the stuff that Osgood's cronies confiscated, remember."

"But not the stuff which Nerys saved," said Josiah, "nor our memories. The opposition think that their cover-up has worked, and we don't need to disillusion them just yet. But we know now what trail we're on, and we'll probably find some more clues when God decides that the time is right. And remember what Carl said about me: 'You stand in the place of the Guardians'. It's my responsibility to act on this."

Bethany leaned back and studied the ceiling. "An ancient history specialist and a political activist. An odd combination. But if the fight you think you're called to take up is really four and a half thousand years old, maybe it makes sense. I guess God will show us the next step in due course…"

Author's Note

So, what's real in the story and what is pure fiction? The ancient maps mystery is a long-standing one which I've been aware of for more than forty years. It comes up time and again in books hypothesizing lost civilizations or alien intervention in our history, hinting strongly at something that doesn't fit with mainstream understanding, yet defying every attempt to create a different picture which holds together.

As a general rule, the specific artefacts handled by the characters in the story are, of necessity to make the novel work, imaginary. The material in the background of the story is real: several maps from supposedly ancient sources are discussed in Maps of the Ancient Sea Kings and elsewhere; the British Museum really does hold a cylinder seal which appears to show Adam and Eve, the tree and the serpent (see Pamphlet 324 from the Creation Science Movement for more details). The Tarxien ship carvings do resemble others that someone from Bethany's background would be aware of. The investigations into Otzi the Iceman are well known, and the Flood / Ice Age model really exists and is the lynchpin that holds my whole concept together. However the 'new' snake carving find which caused Seb and Bethany to go to Tarxien was made up.

Most of the accepted picture of ancient Middle Eastern history derives from the two areas most closely associated with Nimrod and his kin: Mesopotamia and Egypt. I hope that elsewhere there are records from believers in the faith passed down from Noah, waiting to be dug up. Though I invented the Guardians and their records, somewhere Job's journal or Melchizedek's memoirs may still survive, ready to provide independent support for the true history in the Bible. If I can get you thinking about what might be out there, or inspire someone to go and search, I will consider that I've achieved something.

Bibliography

Readers wanting to explore the ideas in the novel further, are referred to the following:

For the development of the 'New' or 'Revised' Chronology for ancient Egypt, see:

1. *Centuries of Darkness: A Challenge to the Conventional Chronology of Old World Archaeology;* Peter James, in collaboration with I.J. Thorpe [et al.]; Rutgers University Press, New Brunswick, NJ., 1993, ISBN 0-8135-1950-0 (hardcover), ISBN 0-8135-1951-9 (paperback); originally published by Jonathan Cape, London, 1991, ISBN 0-224-02647-X

The chronology was popularised, and its implications for our understanding of Old Testament history explored, in:

2. *A Test of Time: The Bible – from Myth to History;* Rohl, David (1995); London: Century. ISBN 0-7126-5913-7. Published in the US as Rohl, David (1995). *Pharaohs and Kings: A Biblical Quest.* New York: Crown Publishers. ISBN 0-517-70315-7.

and

3. *The Lost Testament: From Eden to Exile – The Five-Thousand-Year History of the People of the Bible;* Rohl, David (2002); London: Century. ISBN 0-7126-6993-0. Published in paperback as Rohl, David (2003). *From Eden*

to Exile: The Epic History of the People of the Bible.
London: Arrow Books Ltd. ISBN 0-09-941566-6.

For up to date developments trying to complete the job of reconciling secular and biblical history from Joseph back to the Flood, two researchers worth looking out for are Matt McClellan in Answers Research Journal (online) and Patrick Clarke writing in Journal of Creation. Both of these are technical publications.

The classic source book for the ancient maps hypothesis is:

4. *Maps of the Ancient Sea Kings: Evidence of Advanced Civilization in the Ice Age;* Hapgood, Charles Hutchins; 1966; 1997 Paperback Reprint Edition, Adventures Unlimited Press, ISBN 0-932813-42-9

This has been cited many times by lost civilization and alien contact theorizers, for instance it's the starting point for *Fingerprints of the Gods,* Graham Hancock (1995). I first came across it in a reference in *Man and the Stars,* Duncan Lunan (1974).

The Flood / Ice Age model was promoted in:

5. *An Ice Age Caused by the Genesis Flood;* Michael J Oard (1990); published by the Institute for Creation Research.

For an independent attempt to put forward the idea that the Flood / Ice Age model explains Hapgood's ancient maps hypothesis, see:

6. https://creation.com/images/pdfs/tj/j16_2/j16_2_61-62.pdf (original print version was 2002).

Similar Books from the Publisher

UP
Gary Homewood
978-1-910197-05-9

A hospital.

A small, unassuming ward.

And a dying man who carries a secret with the potential to change the way we view the world.

As Dr Kim Maskell struggles to make sense of the seemingly impossible, he is forced to ask difficult questions. How can he treat a patient whose condition cannot be classified? Should the phenomenon be kept secret or shared with the world? How will this impact the running of the hospital? And most of all...

WHY IS IT HAPPENING?

I, Messiah
Don Southey
978-1-907509-09-4

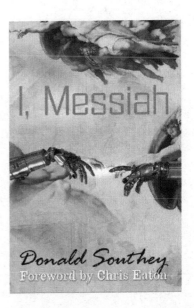

"Only as I took the offered hand, and felt its inhuman coolness, did the truth hit me like an electric shock."

So begins a relationship between a very advanced robot and a very ordinary human that will change their thinking, their lives and their destinies – for ever.